# Consequences of Immature Love

Ray Filby

===========================================

# Consequences of Immature Love

Publisher : Midhurst

Published by Midhurst



This is a work of fiction.

Any resemblance to actual persons, living or dead, is purely coincidental.

Midhurst.
2, Freers Mews,
Warwick,
Warwickshire,
CV34  6DP

# <u>Acknowledgements</u>

The author would like to thank his wife Sue for her encouragement, patience and suggestions during the writing of this story.

The cover picture is a photograph of Blanka Vlasic, the Croatian athlete, taken by Mark Shearman of 'Athletics Images'.

The Bible quote, *'Genesis ch 2 v 7'* is taken from the New International Version.

# Introduction

Boy-Girl, Man-Woman relationships cement our society. Because these relationships are seldom straightforward, they provide scope for an indefinite number of works of fiction. In this novel, you are invited to follow the amorous adventures of Georgina Matthews and Arthur Gray from the time they leave school and start at university until they ultimately marry the partner for whom they seemed destined from the outset.

The story told might be of special interest to a young person embarking on the minefield of love and courtship as they consider the factors which led to the success or failure of the relationships encountered in this novel. Ethical factors are involved and it is significant that a shared Christian faith led to the final happy outcome.

# **Contents**

# Chapter 1

## The Hockey Captain

A coach rolled up the long drive, wending its way between mature azalea and rhododendron bushes. Although it was nearly Easter, most of them were still in full flower. The coach stopped outside a freshly painted Georgian mansion. This was the administration block of St. Ursula's Lady's College, a highly respected girl's public school. This Georgian mansion in front of the school proper, accommodated the offices of the headmistress and senior staff, the school library, the administration offices and the sixth form lounge. The main school building, some twenty yards behind the administration block, was a relatively new edifice which had been built to a very high specification in the 1980's to replace its crumbling predecessor. A covered walkway connected the school and the administration block.

A tall, prim, bespectacled lady in a very smart Dior suit had been waiting outside the imposing entrance to the building, knowing that the coach she was expecting would arrive on time. A slightly shorter but equally smart lady alighted from the coach and the two ladies embraced as they met. They were obviously friends of long standing.

Miss Agnes Trimble was head of St. Ursula's. The lady who had alighted from the coach was Mrs. Mary Brown, head teacher of Mappingham Comprehensive School, a relatively rare single sex state school for girls. Agnes and Mary had become bosom pals from the time they both read greats when at Lady Margaret Hall, Oxford University.

Well behaved girls peered expectantly through the windows of the coach. The visit to St. Ursula's College was one of the high points of the Mappingham School year. An annual hockey match between the two schools at the end of the Spring Term had been inaugurated some ten years earlier when Agnes had discovered that her friend, Mary, had become head of a nearby school. Agnes had always felt uncomfortable that, until she took over St. Ursula's, relationships with other schools had been exclusively with other public schools of similar standing. It was an anathema to Agnes that her girls might grow up, never making contact with girls from less wealthy backgrounds, and perhaps, leaving school under the misapprehension that they were superior to those who went to state schools. Establishing a relationship with a state school was a step towards breaking down these outmoded class barriers.

After the two ladies had exchanged the usual pleasantries, Agnes turned and gestured towards the front door of the college. This was a previously arranged sign for a girl from the school to play her part in the welcome. Adelaide Fitzgerald, a stocky girl with blond hair, neatly combed into a short bob, emerged from the front door. She was dressed in an immaculate Hockey strip, a well pressed white top bearing the emblem of St. Ursula's on the left breast, a pleated maroon skirt and white socks over her shin pads. Adelaide was school hockey captain. Agnes introduced her to Mary (Mrs. Brown), using formal titles of course, and Mary then gestured towards the coach. This was the sign for the Mappingham hockey team, led by their captain, Georgina Matthews, to leave the coach, carrying their sports bags and hockey sticks. Georgina was a tall, slim, amazingly pretty girl whose dark hair was tied in a neat pony-tail. Mary formally introduced Georgina to Agnes (Miss Trimble) and to Adelaide who then led the Mappingham team round the side of the mansion to the spacious school changing rooms.

The hockey team was followed from the coach by Mrs. Edith Pangbourne, a plump woman in a track suit, who led the rest of the girls from the coach. These girls had come as spectators to support the Mappingham team and had earned their places on the coach to be included on this coveted outing by accumulating good behavior and improvement marks during the preceding term. It wasn't just another outing. Absolutely magnificent teas were served up after hockey matches at St. Ursula's. The Mappingham girls were wearing navy blue blazers and grey skirts. The younger girls had fairly new blazers but many of the more senior girls' blazers were distinctly threadbare. Their parents deemed that there was no point in buying new blazers for the final term of school as their daughters would soon be leaving and would be discarding their school uniforms for good. Although school rules required the girls to wear grey skirts, there was no regulation shade of grey and a complete spectrum of greys were on display ranging from nearly black to a pale silver.

Mrs Pangbourne (referred to as Pango by the girls when she was out of earshot) was the head of the Mappingham physical education department and hockey team coach. Mrs. Pangbourne was greeted by Miss Trimble with a friendly handshake as she expressed her hope that the match would prove as exciting as the previous year's encounter. Pango then led the girls along a route, familiar to her from previous visits, round the side of the administration block to the school field where chairs for the visiting supporters had been lined up on one side of the hockey pitch. The St. Ursula girls were already seated on the opposite side of the pitch, excitedly chattering among themselves. They were immaculately turned out in maroon blazers, charcoal skirts, white socks and straw boaters. The impressive coat of arms on the breast pocket of their blazers contrasted with the badges sported on the Mappingham blazers, the letters MGCS (Mappingham Girls Comprehensive School) worked into a simple monogram.

The arrival of the coach, the meeting of the heads, the disembarkation of the team and supporters, and their settling down by the hockey pitch was an annual ritual which took place when the Mappingham hockey team came to St. Ursula's to fulfil this fixture.

The St. Ursula's team were already knocking up on the pitch, rehearsing set pieces and penalty corners. It wasn't long before the Mappingham team emerged from the changing rooms and went to the opposite goal for their pre-match practice. Their strip was a navy top with white sleeves and navy skirt. They didn't wear matching socks.

It was a quintessentially English scene, schoolgirls playing on a well prepared hockey pitch, at the edge of a large playing field area which formed an impressive green carpet stretching to a distant boundary marked by trees and bushes. Rooks cawed noisily as they circled lazily over their rookery in the distant trees while the sweeter sound of songbirds emanated from a nearby hedgerow which ran alongside but ten yards from the hockey pitch where the match was to be played. The main school building, separated from the playing field by a playground marked out with a netball pitch, presided over these recreational areas. Although a relatively new building, no expense had been spared to avoid it appearing as a glass-coated square box like so many ultra-modern buildings, constructed to meet tight economic restrictions. The façade which faced on to the field was the mellow yellowish colour of Cotswold stone. Six impressive ionic columns were evenly spaced across the central part of this frontage beneath a shallow gable and at the top of a wide flight of low rise steps which led to the main entrance between the central columns. Tall rectangular windows pierced the space between each column, with similar windows in the wall which stretched each side of the colonnade to the edge of the building.

After a few minutes, the referee, Miss Olivia Cavendish, clothed in an emerald green tracksuit strode to the middle of the pitch and blew her whistle. Olivia was St. Ursula's hockey coach. The rival captains trotted over to the centre of the pitch and Olivia tossed a coin for Georgina to call. St. Ursula's won the toss and chose ends. The teams took up position and the game started with the standard bully-off.

The teams were evenly matched but St. Ursula's scored first after ten minutes play. St. Ursula's supporters screamed in delight. A few minutes later, Mappingham equalized, eliciting in turn, delighted screams and cheers from their supporters. At half time, St. Ursula's were 3-1 in the lead. Fifteen minutes into the second half, Mappingham closed the gap but the score remained at 3-2 until ten minutes from time. Then Mappingham equalized from a penalty corner. St. Ursula's had always won this fixture and in their determination to win again, they moved most of their defenders into attack. This was a bad tactic. Georgina, Mappingham's captain and central defender picked up the ball just outside the Mappingham penalty area and dribbled down the field. As Mappingham had called most of their forwards back to cope with St. Ursula's extra attacking strength, there was no-one for Georgina to pass to but she'd only one defender to get round. As she approached the defender, she feinted, the defender went the wrong way, and Georgina continued dribbling down the field, hotly pursued by the defender she'd rounded but Georgina was too fast to be caught. She fired a shot when ten yards from goal which the goal-keeper was unable to intercept. Mappingham were now 4-3 in the lead. Only five minutes were now left to play and St. Ursula's desperately tried to equalize but Mappingham held on and some of their players collapsed in relief when the final whistle blew. The captains of each side sportingly called for three cheers for their opponents and then trooped off to the dressing rooms, the intensity of the match having taken a toll on their tired limbs. The Mappingham supporters erupted in delight and cries of 'Georgina, Georgina' echoed from the school building as the supporters acclaimed their hero.

Under the direction of their hockey coaches, the girls from both schools made their way in an orderly fashion to the school dining room where a sumptuous tea had been laid out. Many of the Mappingham girls had been looking forward to the tea rather more than watching the match! The signal for the girls to tuck-in was a short grace, delivered by Miss Trimble. There were neatly cut cucumber and ham sandwiches, sausage rolls, pork pies, chocolate sponge and cream cakes, and a choice of lemonade, coca cola or tea to drink. It was arranged that the girls should not sit in school groups but mingle so that everyone was sitting next to at least one girl from the other school. The meal closed with a couple of short speeches delivered by the opposing captains. Adelaide congratulated the Mappingham team, humorously bemoaning the fact that she would go down in the school annals as the first St. Ursula's hockey captain to lose a match against Mappingham, especially as they had only lost two matches previously during the whole of that hockey season. Georgina responded with a gracious vote of thanks to St. Ursula's for their hospitality in hosting this event, the wonderful tea and the very sportsmanlike way in which the match had been conducted. She commiserated with Adelaide on gaining an unwanted unique achievement but mischievously added that she would go down as the first Mappingham hockey captain ever to win a match against St. Ursula's.

At the end of the tea, the girls said farewell to their new acquaintances and the Mappingham girls loaded on to their coach. Mary Brown was the last one aboard and as she left, she warmly thanked Agnes again for a wonderful afternoon.

"This may surprise you," said Agnes when she knew she was out of earshot from any of the girls, "but just between ourselves, the result of the match was exactly what I'd hoped for. The success of a school doesn't depend on the number of sporting victories it achieves but on the quality, the attitudes and the nature of the girls it turns out. The fact that your girls won the match will perhaps undermine the unfounded sense of superiority that some of my girls display because they come from privileged backgrounds."

With that the heads embraced and Mary joined her girls on the coach.

# Chapter 2

## The School Leaver

It was the last day of the summer term. Mrs. Mary Brown was at her substantial oak desk, seeing to all the extra tasks and details that a head teacher needs to ensure are properly completed at the end of an academic year. She was entering data required by the Local Education Authority into the desktop computer which was used to store so many school records. Her office was tidy, but the many neatly stacked piles of paper arranged on her desk and a nearby table provided the evidence of the number of tasks she was endeavouring to complete before she could relax, and begin to enjoy a well-earned summer break.

She occasionally glanced up at the monitor on the wall of her room. This enabled Mrs. Brown to see what was going on round the school as the closed-circuit television cameras switched from sports hall, to corridor, to stair cases and assembly hall, and to all the other strategic points around the school. She'd even had installed concealed cameras in a couple of classrooms where it was arranged that the more difficult classes would be having their lessons. Yes, even a school like Mappingham had its share of girls who rebelled against discipline, but the staff didn't have to feel that they worked unsupported under a head who shut herself away in an ivory tower. Mrs. Brown was more acquainted than most heads with what was going on around the school. She immediately left her desk to trouble shoot as soon as she became aware of anything untoward going on.

There came the expected knock at the door.

"Come in!" Mrs Brown called out and Georgina Matthews entered.

"Thank you for dropping in Georgina. I asked your head of sixth form to get you to call in before you finally left Mappingham. I just wanted to say what a pleasure it's been to have you as one of my pupils. You've worked hard and excelled, both in your academic work and on the sports field. I'm more than confident that your A-level results will be easily good enough to secure your place at Collingford University. You certainly chose an unusual mix of subjects for your sixth form studies, physics, history and French! Only a very versatile girl like yourself could cope with such diverse disciplines but you've coped very well and your teachers have been more than impressed with the work you have turned in. Your choice of subjects posed quite a problem for Miss Grant who designs the time table but we do try our utmost to see that every girl at Mappingham is able to follow the subjects of her choice in the sixth form.

You could have gone to university to follow an academic career but I can quite understand your opting to train as a physical education teacher. I know that you'll make a great success of your career. Your success in sport, especially athletics and hockey, have been phenomenal. As school hockey captain, you'll be a hard act to follow.

When confronted with some of the antisocial pupils who find their place into all schools, every teacher at some point wonders whether or not they've made the right choice of career, but having the privilege of teaching well motivated pupils passing through our schools makes us realise that we are following a very worth-while career. You've been such a pupil, Georgina, and all of us will be sad, now that you are leaving us for pastures new.

Do keep in touch with us, Georgina. I wish you every success at university."

Georgina blushed at these words of praise from Mrs. Brown.

"Thank you so much for saying all that, Miss, and for making this such a lovely school to be part of. Attending

Mappingham has been a privilege and I hope that I'll live up to your expectations."

Mrs Brown stood up and shook Georgina's hand across the desk. As Georgina left the room and closed the door behind her, Mrs. Brown wiped a tear from her eye.

# Chapter 3

## The Undergaduate

Greg and Julie Matthews had experienced the expected apprehension as their only daughter left the security of home to embark on an independent existence and Georgina had had drummed into her the importance of not getting involved in the drug culture. Second hand stories were related to her of daughters of parents they either knew or had heard of, becoming pregnant during their first term at uni. However, Greg and Julie knew their daughter for the sensible young woman she was and didn't really expect her to get lost down either of these paths.

Georgina found university to be everything she'd hoped for. She was allocated a pleasant study bedroom in one of Collingford University halls of residence and quickly made new friends, both among those living in her hall and those on her course.

As term wore on, identifiable groups of students who were close friends started to form. Georgina's particular group of four young women and an equal number of young men were a very happy group of well-balanced young people, having interests in common, coming from similar backgrounds and laughing at the same sort of jokes. Georgina found herself to be particularly attracted to Jacob, one of the young men in this group. He was handsome, tall and blond. He had a better dress sense than his contemporaries and whenever he spoke, people listened because what he said was invariably sensible. Jacob's speciality was modern languages. He shared Georgina's interest in anything sporting and was often selected to play for the college soccer team. Georgina soon earned a place in the college hockey team.

As the term continued, Jacob and Georgina appeared to be becoming a twosome. They often went on dates together and when the two sports fixture times didn't clash,

Georgina would support Jacob playing soccer while Jacob came to watch Georgina's hockey matches. For Georgina, life seemed absolutely blissful. Having attended a segregated school, Georgina hadn't formed any sort of relationship with boys in Mappingham and was still very naïve in managing boy-girl relationships. Jacob was literally her dream man and she relished every moment she spent in his company.

As the second term at Collingford got underway, Jacob began to sense that Georgina was becoming rather possessive. He felt the time had come to steady down the relationship and broached the matter on one of their dates.

"I think we need to broaden our circle of friends," he suggested to Georgina. "Some the students in my year group are pointing at us as an item and we're far too young be irrevocably linked. We're both under twenty. We've over two more years of study to complete and we need to be free from social ties when it comes to landing the right job. You're a beautiful girl, Georgina, and I do enjoy the times I spend just with you, but I shouldn't be your one and only, exclusive boyfriend. I know that there are lots of fellows who'd like to date you but they've held back from asking because they thought that you were committed to me. It'd be very wrong of me to stand in the way of your experiencing the admiration that other young men besides myself would want to give you. Let's cool it off a bit and date each other less frequently."

Jacob was being eminently sensible and had used a form of words in suggesting that they should slow down the rate at which their relationship was developing which wouldn't be hurtful to Georgina. He hadn't gone so far as suggesting they should completely break off their relationship. However, Georgina felt distraught at what Jacob had said and struggled to hide from Jacob the emotions she was now experiencing. Georgina suspected that Jacob had said all this because there may have been other young women in their group with whom he wished to develop a deeper relationship and she'd be an obstacle to this.

Yes, on the face of it, Jacob was being eminently sensible. However, he too was inexperienced in relating to the opposite sex. Georgina was a young woman with wonderful qualities. A young man might meet such a woman only once in a lifetime. As a result of what he had just said, Jacob would lose Georgina.

Jacob and Georgina separated and went back to their halls of residence. When in the privacy of her room, Georgina broke down and cried for about half an hour. She then started the futile exercise of conjecturing what had gone wrong with their relationship or more particularly, what was wrong with her.

Georgina looked in the mirror.

'Wasn't she pretty enough for Jacob? Were her cheek bones too pronounced? Was there something wrong with her figure? Was she too thin?'

Georgina had no need to worry on that score. She was certainly very slim but not to the point of being considered thin although, because of her keenness to excel at sport, she had trained hard and carried no surplus fat. She had well developed shoulders and muscular definition in her arms. Her abdominal muscles similarly showed pronounced definition. She had not adorned her body with tattoos which Georgina considered to be a disfigurement.

'Perhaps Jacob preferred plumper girls with completely smooth bodies like Alison,' thought Georgina, mentally comparing herself to another girl in their circle. Unlike Georgina, Alison had large breasts. 'Is this really what men are looking for?' she wondered.

Georgina knew she had shapely legs with well-formed calf muscles and delicate ankles from which the bones in her feet could be seen radiating to her toes. Perhaps that was the trouble, she was too bony! Her collar bones were prominent but delicate, but her lower ribs were pronounced, standing out above the point where her body tapered to a slender waist.

Georgina was wide of the mark. Jacob had never seen Georgina in a bikini to be aware of these features over which Georgina was now agonizing. Had he done so, he would have recognized that Georgina's figure was almost perfect. The truth of the matter was that Georgina had a face and a figure which wouldn't have looked out of place on a Pirelli calendar or a Victoria's Secret lingerie catalogue. Georgina wasn't fully aware that the attractiveness of a woman to a man was not wholly dependent on the beauty of her face or the perfection of her figure, but here again, Georgina scored well in other important qualities. In addition to having a lovely face and figure, Georgina had the attractive qualities of intelligence, love, humour and selflessness which were far more important than mere physical beauty.

Jacob had been foolish not to take more account of these.

The following morning, Georgina had recovered her composure and was feeling much better about herself. Her group of friends continued to mix happily and enjoy each other's company. Her relationship with Jacob cooled off quite a bit although she still went out on the occasional date with him. However, their relationship was no longer exclusive. Georgina was also able to enjoy dates with other students.

Another man was soon to come into Georgina's life.

# Chapter 4

## The Older Man

The academic year moved on. Only a short term remained for the students who'd allowed busy social lives to cause them to drop behind in their studies, to put in that extra spurt of work and catch up well enough to succeed in their summer exams.

When the students returned after the Easter break, the hockey goals had been put away in store for the following season and the pitch within the running track had been remarked out to define the javelin and discus landing region and distance circles.

Athletics came second only to hockey in the sports Georgina loved. She was very competitive, trained hard and soon caught the eye of the athletics training staff at the university as someone who might have a future in athletics. She should certainly have a place in the college athletics team. Georgina was a good all round athlete in the mould of the hept-athlete, Jennifer Ennis-Hill. Slight as she was, discus, javelin and shot putt all came within her repertoire but her specialities were the high jump and short distance running events.

One of the big events for the university on the women's athletics calendar was the annual match against the Corinthian Ladies AC, a well reputed sports club whose track was located on the edge of Collingford. Georgina had been selected to represent the college in the high jump and 400 m in this contest.

Two university mini-buses conducted the ladies' athletics team to the Corinthian athletics stadium. They were shown to a suite of impressive and spacious changing rooms where they prepared themselves for the match. A good crowd of spectators had gathered and were occupying the seats in the stand.

For most events, two university students competed against a pair of athletes from the

Corinthian club. The Corinthian ladies were really dedicated athletes and the university only picked up a handful of first and second places.

In the high jump event, the Collingford University second string dropped out when the bar reached 1.45 m but Georgina battled it out with the two Corinthian ladies until one failed at 1.65 m. Georgina and the remaining lady struggled at 1.70 m. The Corinthian athlete failed at her third attempt and it was finally down to Georgina to clinch the competition with her third jump. She just cleared it to achieve her personal best and give the University some badly needed points on the board. The bar was raised to 1.75 m but this was just beyond Georgina's capabilities. Her performance was very creditable, especially when compared with the U.K. national record of 1.95 m. The world record of 2.09 m seems unattainable. It was made by an Eastern European athlete at the World Championships held in Rome in 1987 before the International Athletics Federation was as intent as it is now in checking for drug abuse.

The final event before the relay was the 400 m. Georgina was drawn in the outside lane. The gun set the race off and Georgina had a good start. Because the start was staggered, Georgina had no idea where her rivals were until she rounded the final bend. She then realized that the Corinthian lady drawn on the inside lane was just ahead and she struggled to close the small gap between them before breasting the tape. She didn't quite make it. The Corinthian lady won in the creditable time of 52.1 s. Georgina was timed at 52.3 s, another personal best. The national record and world records for this event stood at 49.43 and 47.6 s. The world record was achieved by an East German athlete at a World Cup event in Australia in 1985.

As Georgina put on her tracksuit at the end of the event, she was approached by a gentleman, smartly dressed in a suit and tie. He introduced himself as Michael (call me

Mike) Forbes and explained that he was the main sponsor of the Corinthian Ladies AC. He commented on how impressed he'd been with Georgina's performances that evening and pointed out that Marcia Jones, the athlete who had won the 400 m race, was on the verge of being selected for Great Britain's Olympic team. Mike considered that Georgina seemed to be not far off achieving this sort of level herself and suggested that if she joined the Corinthian Ladies AC, their professional coaches might enable her to achieve this. He invited Georgina to meet for a dinner date at 'the Spanish Ambassadors' Restaurant' to discuss this further. The Spanish Ambassadors' was just about the most prestigious restaurant in Collingford.

At 7:30 p.m. the following Tuesday, Georgina found herself arriving at the Spanish Ambassadors'. As a student, she hadn't any specially fine clothes to wear for the occasion but she'd a very nice dress which she considered to be sufficiently presentable. Mike was already waiting for her at the entrance of the plush foyer of this establishment, dressed in a smart dinner jacket and tuxedo. The restaurant was softly illuminated by a set of quite spectacular chandeliers. Everything here was of the highest quality. The tastefully patterned carpet had a thick pile. The tables were laid with damask table cloths, silver cutlery, bone china plates and cut glass wine glasses. The waiters were immaculately turned out in evening dress. One of them conducted Mike and Georgina to a table for two at the edge of this restaurant,

Georgina was handed a menu in a leather binding. The names of the dishes were boldly printed in French but this gave Georgina no trouble as she had taken a French A-level. In any case, English translations of each dish were given in smaller print below the main titles. No prices were listed on the menu that Georgina had been handed so she had no idea of how much this was going to cost but she realized that the meal was not going to come cheap. Georgina selected salmon soufflé as a starter and pork medallions for her main course. Mike chose a prawn cocktail starter and a beef steak for his main course. Mike accepted the Maitre d'Hotel's recommendation of an excellent red wine, a fruity shiraz.

This was Georgina's first opportunity to assess what Mike was like. Although smartly dressed, he was not particularly handsome. She placed his age as coming in the mid-forties range. He spoke with a cultured accent with just a hint of home-counties, probably Essex. It was quite clear that he wasn't short of money.

Mike took great interest in what Georgina was doing - her sporting prowess, her ambition to be a physical education teacher and her home background. He eulogized over the Corinthian Ladies AC as one of the finest, if not the finest, ladies athletics clubs in the country. It had produced a number of Olympians and with the right coaching, he considered that Georgina might join this elite group.

"If you ever represented Great Britain in the Olympics," he declared, "every school in the country would want you as a member of their physical education staff. You could have the pick of the best schools in England, Scotland or Wales."

Georgina fell for this persuasion and agreed to join the Corinthian Ladies AC.

Mike told Georgina very little about himself. He was now single but had had a brief marriage which ended fifteen years ago.

"It was a great mistake," he explained. "We were totally incompatible but I didn't realize this until we were actually married. We got divorced by mutual consent."

Mike said very little about what he did, simply describing himself as a financial consultant in the employ of a number of city businesses. It was clear to Georgina that whatever this work involved, it was extremely well paid.

At the end of the meal, Mike drove Georgina back to university in his gleaming blue Jaguar which had been parked just behind the restaurant in the Spanish Ambassadors' car park. Georgina felt flattered when Mike suggested that they should meet again at a different high class restaurant the following Tuesday.

# Chapter 5

## The Wife

Georgina and Mike met quite frequently over the next few weeks. Their rendezvous was always a first class restaurant, sometimes in Collingford but very often at one of the five-star hotels in the more fashionable villages around Collingford.

Georgina joined the Corinthian Ladies AC and soon impressed their coaches, not just with her natural ability, but her dedication to training. She represented the club in matches against other similar athletics clubs and always gave a good account of herself. If Georgina found there was a clash between the athletics events at the university and the Corinthian Ladies AC, the university always took preference in Georgina's decision on whom she should represent. Georgina also built up a new circle of friends at the athletics club, none of whom seemed to be jealous of Georgina's success but were very supportive and encouraging, especially when the

Corinthians were competing against another club. Although he was obviously well known to all the members of the club, Georgina found it strange that none of them were prepared to talk much about Mike.

As Georgina and Mike continued to meet, things began to take an ominous turn. Mike started to buy Georgina presents which he gave her during the course of their dates, really expensive presents. She received diamond brooches, sapphire bracelets, an emerald necklace and a Rolex Cosmograph watch. Georgina looked up the value of this on the Rolex website and found that its value was not far short of £10,000! Georgina felt embarrassed but flattered that she was receiving such wonderful gifts from a man who obviously adored her.

Occasionally, when Georgina had a free afternoon, Mike would drive her out for tea and cakes at his house in Glenstone Parva, a fashionable village not far from Collingford. As one might expect, this was magnificent. It was a five bedroom mansion of mock

Tudor design set in a quiet cul-de-sac. Neat gardens with manicured lawns and colourful flowerbeds were laid out to the front and the rear of the house. The driveway was a block-paved semicircle at the front of the house from which there was access to a double garage, although Mike only had one car, his powerful Jaguar. The house was surrounded by shrubs, mainly azaleas, rhododendrons and hibiscus in front of a curtain of conifers, so the house was hardly overlooked by neighbours. Mike explained that he had to employ a gardener two days a week to keep everything in good order.

Mike's living room, where he served tea, was decorated in Regency style and laid out with good quality furniture, appropriate to the period, although Mike explained that the items were not expensive antiques but modern furniture manufactured to a Regency design. Tea invariably consisted of pre-prepared sandwiches and cream cakes, served from an expensive bone china tea service manufactured by Royal Doulton.

The silver teapot was apparently a genuine antique and described by Mike as 'Louis the 14th'.

It was during one of these afternoon tea parties that Mike raised the issue of sex but Georgina was very highly principled and quite capable of forcefully expressing her opinions.

"Sex is for marriage," she asserted. "If I were to have sex with you now, I would feel like a prostitute who'd been bought with the expensive gifts you've given me."

As the relationship continued, Mike continued to buy Georgina expensive gifts including driving lessons and a Ford Ka. Whenever Mike broached the subject of sex again, Georgina always gave the same answer. In the end, Mike proposed marriage.

"We can't begin to consider this," said Georgina "until we know much more about each other's backgrounds. You have never met my parents and I know nothing whatsoever about your parents, or indeed, any of your relatives or friends outside the Corinthian Athletic Club."

Mike explained that he was an only child of parents who'd long since died. He believed he had aunts and uncles but had only met them when he was a very young child and he'd no idea of their current whereabouts or even their names.

Georgina arranged for Mike to come and meet her parents.

Greg and Julie were disturbed by their daughter's relationship with Mike. Their chief cause for concern was the age difference. It was quite true to say that Mike was old enough to be Georgina's father. Indeed, it was possible that he was older than Greg. While they appreciated the fact that Mike would be able to amply provide for their daughter's welfare, they were very concerned that so little was known about

Mike, exactly what he did for a living and his family background.

Without letting Georgina know, Greg contacted a private enquiry agent to discover as much as he could about Mike. The enquiry agent was quickly able to provide information on Mike's background. This is something which Greg could have probably done himself, had he known a bit more about using the Internet and gone into the Somerset House website.

Yes, Mike was the only son of deceased parents. He'd been divorced by mutual consent fifteen years earlier after a very short marriage. Names of aunts and uncles could be obtained but since it appeared that none of these had seen Mike since he was a small child, they wouldn't be able to add appreciably to this basic information and so it didn't seem worthwhile locating them. In order to find more about Mike's work, the enquiry agency would need to arrange a discreet tail on Mike and the cost of this service was more than Greg was prepared to pay. On the face of it, everything Mike had told Georgina about himself held up.

Georgina agreed to marry Mike. She liked him rather than loved him but there were a number of factors which pushed her in the direction of this particular marriage. Security is something which only the very foolish don't consider when contemplating marriage and this was something Georgina would gain from being married to a very wealthy man. Being able to live in such a gorgeous mansion also featured among the pro's when Georgina looked at the advantages and disadvantages of marrying Mike. However, security and wealth aren't the most important considerations in planning to get married.

Although neither Georgina nor her family had been church goers, they wanted a church wedding. Mike would have preferred a civil ceremony but he was prepared to follow Georgina's wishes. Problems divorcees experienced in the past in seeking to be married in church were no longer such an obstacle in this day and age.

So it was, Georgina and Mike married on an April's day during Georgina's final year at university. The wedding was a very happy, well attended occasion. Georgina's close friends from college were all there including Jacob. There were very few guests from what might be regarded as Mike's side. Most of Georgina's friends from the Corinthian Ladies AC declined the invitation.

# Chapter 6

## The Divorcee

Marriage to Mike didn't turn out quite as Georgina had expected or hoped. After an Easter holiday honeymoon in Salerno on the Amalfi coast of Italy, Mike and Georgina returned to their lovely home in Glenstone Parva. Now that they were actually married, Mike did not provide Georgina with the companionship she expected. Their sex life was good but in the evenings, Mike was far more concerned with watching television than engaging in conversation. Anyway, Georgina had a lot of course work to keep her busy in the evenings and she certainly enjoyed being mistress of this really magnificent home.

After a couple of weeks, Mike announced that a lot of work had recently come up without exactly explaining the nature of this work. This work would mean that he had to spend quite a bit of time away from home.

Sometimes, he would be unable to return home in the evening.

Georgina accepted that to earn the type of money that Mike was being paid, working unsociable hours would be part of the deal. Georgina concentrated on her studies and attended the Corinthian Ladies AC for training at least once a week.

On one of these training evenings, one of the other girls at the club suggested that Georgina should find out what was going on at 5, Berring's Way or the St. George's Hotel in Yarnmarket, a town quite near Collingford. Georgina could elucidate no more information from her friend but realized what was being implied.

The following day after lectures at college were finished, Georgina drove to Yarnmarket and located the St. George's Hotel. She realised that she would have to be careful in her investigation and worked out a strategy. She approached the reception desk and enquired if Mr. Forbes was expected to be staying there that evening. Georgina was quite shocked with the revelation that followed. It appeared that Mike had a permanently booked suite with a double room. No, he wasn't in today but was expected next Tuesday. He stayed at the Hotel usually about once a fortnight and was usually accompanied by his wife when he stayed there.

Georgina declined to leave her name. To avoid the receptionist letting Mike know that someone had been enquiring after him, she told the receptionist that there was no need to leave a message for Mr. Forbes. She'd called at the hotel because she'd just missed Mr. Forbes who'd left work earlier than she'd expected but that the matter wasn't so urgent that it couldn't wait until she saw him at the office tomorrow.

Mike had told Georgina that he wouldn't be home that evening. If he wasn't going to be at home and wasn't expected at the St. George's Hotel, perhaps she should investigate 5, Berring's Way. Berring's Way was in the bed-sit area on the edge of Collingford.

Georgina drove in her Ford Ka to Berring's Way and parked it round a corner so that it wouldn't be obvious for anyone driving into Berring's Way, but it was in a position which secured a vantage point from which Georgina could observe all that was going on outside No. 5. She'd arrived there at 7 o'clock and prepared herself for a long wait, possibly an all-night vigil. Georgina didn't have to wait too long. At about ten past eight, Mike's Jaguar purred up the street and parked where there was a gap between the parked cars a few doors down from No. 5. Mike alighted from the car and went to the other side to open the door for his passenger. From the car emerged Jacqueline, a girl Georgina recognized as a member of the Corinthian Ladies AC. They made their way to No. 5. Jacqueline withdrew a key from her purse and they went inside. The door closed behind them.

What was Georgina to do? She remained in the car for another half hour. She decided that it wouldn't be a good idea to march up to the house, knock at the door and confront her errant husband there and then. Neither was there any point in spending an uncomfortable night in her small car outside the house. What would she do when Mike finally emerged, perhaps late morning the following day? Georgina decided to return home, get some sleep and confront Mike the following evening, the time he'd told her that he'd be back from work.

The following evening when Georgina returned home from college, she ensconced herself in the living room and waited for Mike's return. Mike came in at about 5 o'clock, went over to kiss Georgina, asked if she had had a good day, sat in his own chair and started to open the newspaper which Georgina had left on the table beside his chair after it had been delivered that morning.

"Did you have a good time last night?" Georgina asked.

Mike looked up, a slight shade of alarm on his face. This wasn't something Georgina usually asked and there was a harshness in her tone.

"Yes, OK." Mike replied, "Why?"

"Was Jaqueline a good lie?" Georgina challenged.

Mike really looked uncomfortable now. He said nothing but just shifted uncomfortably in his seat.

"Who are these wives who stay with you at St. George's Hotel?" Georgina continued.

Mike started to feel really uncomfortable. Whatever had Georgina discovered? How did she know about all this? What could he say?

"These are just women I spend time with when I can't be with you."

"Nonsense. I was here last night."

"Every man needs to spend some time with women other than his wife. It's just a thing men do!"

"Not true and it's certainly not going to be true in the case of a man to whom I'm married!"

Mike had nothing more to say. He stood up and quickly walked out of the room. That night, Georgina slept in a bed in one of the spare rooms.

During the days that followed, heated discussions flared up between them as they considered the future of their relationship as a married couple.

"I don't want the father of my children sleeping with other women!"

"I don't want children!"

This was obviously something which should have been discussed before they got married. Their differences were irreconcilable. Mike wasn't prepared to change his lifestyle. Georgina wasn't prepared to remain married to a serial adulterer. Georgina expressed her intention of divorcing Mike.

"On what grounds do you intend to divorce me?" asked Mike.

"Your adultery," replied Georgina.

"If you try to divorce me on those grounds," said Mike, "I'll contest it."

"What chance do you have of winning your case?" challenged Georgina. "I know you've slept with Jacqueline. I know that you've slept with, I don't know how many women, at St. George's Hotel."

"I have the resources to hire a very able and expensive lawyer," countered Mike. "To prove adultery, you have to have corroborated evidence of dates, names and times. Even the hotel won't be able to provide you with this evidence. A long drawn out legal case will cost you money you don't have. However, I am prepared to consider an uncontested divorce on the grounds of mutual incompatibility."

Georgina considered this. She didn't want a long drawn out proceeding with unsavoury details appearing in the papers. Some mud would probably stick to her although this would be quite unjustified. What Mike had said was true. She didn't have the financial resources to fight him in court and it was unlikely that she would be granted legal aid. She therefore agreed to make incompatibility the ground on which they would mutually sue for divorce.

Georgina naturally had to seek the guidance of a solicitor in making arrangements for this divorce and her solicitor was very interested in Mike's financial affairs. Apart from knowing that he must have a good income, Georgina had no idea of what that income was, what work he actually did and who were Mike's employers. Her solicitor pointed out that as his legal wife, she would have a financial claim on Mike's wealth. He thought she'd have had a good chance to sue for divorce on the grounds of Mike's adultery when she could make an even more substantial claim against Mike. He pointed out that this was probably the reason that Mike wanted the divorce to be on grounds of mutual incompatibility rather than on his adultery. The solicitor's advice was to sue Mike for all she could get.

Georgina would have none of this. She didn't want to go down as one of the breed of young women who marry an older man and then get divorced to claim a large slice of their former spouse's property. She just wanted a quick divorce.

It was now the summer holiday period. Georgina had qualified as a teacher of physical education and had secured a post at Kelvinborough Comprehensive School where she would serve her probationary year. Kelvinborough was a town, thirty or so miles from Collingford. Georgina packed her bags from the house at Glenstone Parva and moved into a flat in Kelvinborough at the earliest opportunity. She made a point of leaving all the valuable jewelry that Mike had given her on the kitchen table in Mike's house. The only thing she kept was the Ford Ka. She knew that she'd need her own transport to maintain an independent existence.

The divorce went through without a hitch and a decree nisi was granted which in turn became a decree absolute. Georgina now felt free to start a completely new phase in her life. She dropped her married name and from the time she started at her new school, she was known as Miss Matthews.

# Chapter 7

## The Probationary Teacher

Kelvinborough School was a run of the mill comprehensive school. Georgina felt uneasy as she settled into the staff room although it was difficult to pinpoint any particular problem. Mrs. Josephine (Jo) Smith, the head of physical education under whom Georgina worked, was pleasant enough. She didn't take to Mr. Bronson, the headmaster, but then, she didn't have to have much dealing with him. Mr. Bronson seldom moved from his office. Some of the staff were very nice indeed, especially Ben Hardy, the head of the physics department and Ken Campbell, one of the English teachers. Georgina really took exception to one teacher, Stan (Stinky) Silvester, head of the chemistry department. Stinky was a nickname, not exclusively used by the children to refer to the head of the chemistry department while out of earshot. He had the reputation of always getting exceptionally good exam results and he lauded this over the rest of the staff. At their first meeting, he sneered at Georgina as a physical education teacher who had a cushy number because she wasn't going to be judged on exam results.

Not only was there something wrong at Kelvinborough School but Georgina was no longer the innocent, idealistic young woman who'd entered university three years earlier. She now had a failed marriage behind her and something had rubbed off on Georgina as a result of that experience which undermined her previous impeccable moral integrity. While there is no doubt that the main blame for the failure of the marriage rested with Mike, Georgina had a share in the responsibility for that. She'd married a man she knew very little about, motivated by material considerations rather than love.

Through listening to staff gossip, Georgina discovered one of the very unpleasant things that went on at Kelvinborough School. A large number of field trips were organized and it seemed that some of the male staff who supervised these trips used them as an opportunity to have inappropriate relationships with the sixth form girls who went. Some of these men were married. They were gambling their careers and marriages on the expectation that these misdemeanours would never come to light. Although the girls concerned may have boasted about what went on to their friends, their parents would be kept in the dark about the true nature of the field trips their daughters had attended.

Georgina settled into her teaching routine well. The kids at Kelvinborough were OK. The school had a relatively affluent catchment area and a large number of the children were very keen on sport. When interviewed for the job, Georgina's interest and success in hockey and athletics had been identified and as a result, Georgina was given responsibility for coaching the school hockey teams and the girls' athletics teams. The boys didn't play hockey but soccer which was well catered for by the school.

The school had excellent sports facilities with two well-equipped sports halls. Jo Smith had a large room leading off the main sports hall. The other large room leading off this hall was shared by the two male physical education teachers. Georgina had a separate large room which adjoined the smaller of the two sports halls. These rooms were ideal as teacher's changing rooms and as there was a large desk in each, they also served as offices for Jo and Georgina.

As any teacher knows, a probationary year is a very busy and challenging time. Georgina had no time to develop interests outside school and had to rely on the staff at the school for male company. She formed a particular attachment to Ken Campbell. They had similar interests. Ken had played hockey at university and organized the school cross country teams. Although he taught English, Ken was a history graduate and history had been one of Georgina's A level subjects. As they grew closer in their relationship, Ken confided to Georgina that his marriage was going through a difficult patch. Yes, Georgina could empathise with this. Ken bemoaned the fact that he was continually nagged at home. He could do nothing right. He was concerned that the continuing rowing between himself and his wife was having a bad effect on the children whom he loved dearly.

Georgina and Ken became conscious that other staff were becoming concerned that the relationship between the two of them was becoming quite intense. They therefore decided that rather than have their tete-a-tetes in the staff room, they would meet in Georgina's changing room. However, they had to be discreet in the way they did this. They would only meet during their free periods when Jo was working in another part of the school. Ken would find a way of approaching the sports hall so that his destination wouldn't be recognised by other members of staff.

After a while, as their relationship became even more intense, and thinking that their strategy of secrecy was working, they went too far. Occasionally, Georgina returned to her changing room dressed in the skimpy kit that she sometimes wore for teaching in the sports hall. Gym mats were usually laid out on the floor of Georgina's office. When Ken and Georgina were together in Georgina's room, they would lock the door. The combination of temptation and opportunity can defeat even the most devout individuals. Inevitably, Ken and Georgina ended up making love together. They were both naïve if they thought they could get away with this without anyone knowing what was going on and Georgina became aware that Jo was starting to show a certain degree of hostility towards her.

One day when they met, Ken's face was very grave. He told Georgina that his wife knew that he was having an inappropriate relationship with a member of staff at school although she didn't know it was Georgina. Ken's wife had issued an ultimatum that unless he moved to another school, she would divorce him. For the sake of the children, Ken didn't want this to happen. He had therefore sent off applications to a number of schools. Their relationship would have to come to an end. Georgina was now more emotionally resilient than in the days when her relationship with Jacob had faltered. She sadly accepted the situation for what it was and wished Ken success in his quest for a new post.

Three weeks later, Ken announced that he was moving to a new school on the edge of London where he had been offered the post of head of the English department.

Ken was a popular member of staff and a substantial collection was made to buy him a really nice leaving present. The presentation was made on the last day of term by the head of the English department. Mr. Bronson didn't usually get involved in these rites of passage. The occasion was a happy one although Georgina obviously felt sad that she'd be losing a colleague to whom she'd grown very close, too close.

However, the farewell event was marred when Ken's wife, Mrs. Campbell, burst in at the end of the presentation and speeches. She issued a tirade against the staff at the school.

"Some of the women here are no more than sluts," she ranted "'and from what I hear, some of you men are even worse."

It was with some relief that Georgina heard 'women' referred to in the plural. Mrs Campbell did not know which particular teacher had had an affair with her husband.

Mrs Campbell carried on for about quarter of an hour, generally decrying the staff and denouncing the staff room as a den of iniquity. Indeed, to be realistic, as far as some of the staff were concerned, what she was saying had the ring of truth. She then stormed out, followed by an embarrassed Ken Campbell. For a while, silence descended on the staff room. With a wife like that, some of the staff could see why Ken had sought love elsewhere and the moral burden lay with him rather than with the new young teacher they believed he had seduced.

The silence was broken by Miss McDonald who taught home economics. She declared, "What else should one expect of a Campbell?"

The jibe was directed at Mrs. Campbell rather than the unfortunate Ken.

Thus ended Georgina's probationary year at Kelvinborough Comprehensive School.

# Chapter 8

## The Junior Wrangler

Arthur Gray was a bright young man, very bright. Tall, fair-haired, handsome and athletic, Arthur had a lot going for him. Some even described him as a lookalike of the football star, David Beckham! Although from a state school, he'd won an open scholarship to King's College, Cambridge, to read mathematics. King's College had been founded by Henry VI, primarily to further educate boys from Eton College, a school which he had also founded. Arthur was exceptional in being a state educated student attending that college.

Arthur loved maths and his ambition was to become a teacher who could hopefully make maths exciting to pupils who had been turned off by the subject. He had a further ambition of being able to contribute to the development of a poor nation by enlisting as a teacher in a developing country, perhaps somewhere in Africa or Asia.

University life suited Arthur well. His special friends were Paul Musgrove and Arnold Cochrane. Because of the superficial similarity of their names, Arthur, Paul and Arnold, to Athos, Porthos and Aramis, the trio became known as the Three Musketeers. They shared a vibrant Christian faith and when not worshipping in their college chapels, they attended Christ Church in Christchurch Street, located just south of the River Cam. All three of them played soccer for their respective college teams and were actively involved in a range of college activities and societies including the Christian Union where they had first met.

Although they spent a lot of time together, Paul was often absent from their company as he had a girlfriend, Helen, who was reading geography at Girton College. Helen also attended Christ Church on a regular basis. Arnold, perhaps rather like the fictional Aramis, seemed to be particularly attractive to women. He had a number of girlfriends but was not attached to anyone in a serious way. Arthur enjoyed female company but tended to keep women at arm's length. He was wary about forming any particular attachments. This may have been due to his having a long term ambition in which a wife did not feature.

Even in this enlightened age, some of the Cambridge colleges were very male dominated and the 'Three Musketeers' took the opportunity afforded by college dances, which were attended by local girls as well as female university students, to escape this segregated environment.

At one of these dances, Arthur's attention became focused on a very pretty girl who had come with a group of friends. She was tall, slim, blue-eyed and blond. Her hair had been exquisitely coiffured and her long blue dress had been beautifully tailored. Arthur asked her for a dance and discovered that her name was Alice Manders. They spent the rest of the evening together and Arthur walked her home. She didn't live far from the city centre.

Meeting Alice completely changed Arthur's wariness about becoming involved with a girlfriend. Arthur and Alice started to spend a great deal of time together. Alice seemed delighted to have a university student as a regular boyfriend and Arthur was entranced by the beauty of this young woman. Alice became what might be described as a trophy girlfriend. Whenever they attended a party, Alice was always by far the prettiest girl in the room. When they walked down the street, passers-by would think, 'what a lucky fellow to have such a girl in tow'.

However, after the euphoria of physical attraction began to subside, Arthur realized that there was a downside to their relationship. They really had very little in common. It was difficult for Arthur to strike up a stimulating conversation with Alice. She always just agreed with everything Arthur said. Arthur took her to Christ

Church and discovered that Alice had a remarkably good singing voice but if he attempted to talk about spiritual things, she just passively listened and appeared to have neither a viewpoint nor an understanding of what he was talking about. Arthur came to the conclusion that Alice came to church just because she knew he wanted her to but wasn't really interested in developing a meaningful faith. Alice was keen on pop music and this was an area where Alice's knowledge far exceeded Arthur's as his taste leaned towards the classical and romantic composers.

Arthur was one of those people who thought in terms of how the long term future might work out. He could really see that Paul and Helen had the prospect of a really wonderful long-term future together. Although Helen wasn't particularly pretty, she was attractive enough and more importantly, she had a very keen mind. Her faith was sound and she could eloquently express the basis for her beliefs. As a couple, they would be an asset to any church they attended. Arthur wanted a relationship like this for himself.

Arnold had so many girlfriends. Arthur hoped that he wouldn't be a philanderer all his life. He wondered just what sort of girl would Arnold end up with on a long-term basis?

Arthur's thoughts turned to his relationship with Alice. Not only was she very pretty, she was a really nice person. She obviously felt very attached to Arthur. Arthur's Christian life was very important to him and he wanted a long-term partner who would share in this to the full. He realised with a heavy heart that Alice would just not fill this role. Although she had so many wonderful qualities, Alice was not another Helen. What could he do, now that his relationship had developed so far? He didn't have the heart to just coldly break it off. The solution to Arthur's problem came from an unexpected quarter.

Arnold was a very perceptive young man. He realised that the warmth of Arthur's relationship with Alice was rapidly draining and he broached the matter with Arthur. He admitted to Arthur that he had been watching Alice carefully and had found her to be not just pretty but far more attractive in many other ways than any of the many girls with whom he consorted. However, until recently, he had always assumed that she and Arthur were very much an exclusive twosome. He now had the distinct feeling that Arthur did not want the relationship to continue.

On a whim, Arthur asked Arnold if he would like to date Alice. Arnold was taken aback at first. He indicated that he had not taken this step before because of her relationship with Arthur whom he regarded as one of his best friends. Arthur told Arnold that he had correctly diagnosed the situation between himself and Alice. He said that he would discuss the situation with Alice and he hoped that would clear the way for Arnold to arrange a date with her.

When they next met up, Arthur told Alice that he had a friend who found her very attractive and would like to arrange to date her but hadn't done so because he believed that he and Alice had an exclusive relationship. Alice asked Arthur who this friend was. He told her it was Arnold and Arthur felt a little humiliated when Alice's eyes lit up and declared that she would really like a date with Arnold. This realignment had been easier for Arthur than he had expected. He had overestimated Alice's devotion to himself but the outcome of this conversation meant that he could recede from his relationship with Alice without causing her the heartbreak that he had feared.

So it was, Alice became Arnold's girlfriend and they soon seemed deliriously happy together. Over the next weeks and months, Arthur observed from the sidelines the way the relationships of his two friends were developing. In a sense, they both flourished. Paul became engaged to Helen and a short time later, Arnold and Alice announced their engagement. However, Arthur noticed that while Paul and Helen became more and more of a key couple in the way Christ Church developed its ministry of outreach to the Cambridge community, Arnold's association with Christ Church dwindled. Arnold and Alice still attended church together but, it seemed, only on an occasional basis.

At the end of their three years at Cambridge, the 'Three Musketeers' all graduated with good degrees which they'd be able to convert to MA's. in due course without the need to take further examinations. Arthur did particularly well. The mathematics exams at Cambridge University are known as Tripos and the student who comes out top is known as the Senior Wrangler. The student who comes second is entitled the Junior Wrangler. To come first or second in these exams is a mark of considerable mathematical ability.

The university dons who set these papers sometimes include a classical problem which the students are unlikely to have encountered before and which had never previously been solved. Occasionally, the best of these examinees produce a valid solution to the problem while working under the pressurized conditions of a competitive examination!

The students who come lower down in the list, while still earning first class honours degrees, are known as the $3^{rd}$ Wrangler, $4^{th}$ Wrangler and so on. An interesting situation arose when the university broke from its mediaeval roots and allowed women to become full members of the university. Women doing well in the mathematics Tripos were not given the title of Wrangler but if they came $6^{th}$, for example, they were allocated the honour of coming 'Between the $5^{th}$ and $6^{th}$ Wrangler'! The university have continued with this outmoded system as part of its tradition but found one year that they had to award a woman a particularly rare distinction. She came top in the Tripos and had to be awarded the title, 'Above the Senior Wrangler'! This is an honour no man could hope to achieve!

Arthur came second in the Tripos examination and thus became Junior Wrangler for the year. The university authorities tried to persuade Arthur not to proceed with a teaching career in schools but to stay on and do research. Becoming Junior Wrangler was quite a distinction and a promising academic career lay ahead. However, Arthur had already planned his future.

The time had come for the 'Three Musketeers' to separate and start new phases of their lives.

Paul and Helen got married two weeks after their graduation and embarked on post-graduate courses at Durham University. Arthur was Paul's best man at the wedding. A month later, Arnold and Alice got married and moved to London where Arnold joined an accountancy firm, expecting in due course to become a fully-fledged chartered accountant.

Arthur remained at Cambridge to complete a post-graduate certificate of education (PGCE). He fulfilled his probationary year as a teacher at a comprehensive school in Bristol.

# Chapter 9

## The Head of the Mathematics Department

Arthur did really well in his probationary year in overcoming a problem common to teachers of mathematics. A large number of school pupils find mathematics a complete turn off. They have to struggle to master skills which they'll apparently never need again in real life, just to pass an examination, and then they can forget most of the maths they ever learned. Arthur was able to go someway towards meeting the challenge this posed by building projects into his teaching which not only satisfied the curriculum requirements but illustrated the application of maths in real life situations. The pupils could recognize that these projects related to things that they were interested in and saw that they weren't abstract but would have a future practical significance for themselves.

Arthur needed his career to move on quickly and he applied for and secured the post of head of mathematics at Kelvinborough Comprehensive School. This was a remarkable achievement for someone who had only just completed his probationary teaching year but good mathematicians are in short supply in the teaching profession. Arthur's success in his teaching had earned him really good references and the distinction of being Junior Wrangler weighed heavily in his favour.

The teacher in-service training day at the beginning of the new term at Kelvinborough enabled Arthur to get to know some of his colleagues. The staff in his department were a pleasant enough group of young men and women. Arthur's reputation had gone before him and they were expectant rather than apprehensive about working under a new departmental head. None of these teachers were involved in the infamous field trips where rumours of serious professional misconduct were said to take place.

During the day, Arthur had a one-to-one meeting with Mr. Bronson, the head-teacher. His office was sparse and his desk was completely clear. Was this a measure of a high degree of efficiency or did Mr. Bronson just delegate all his work?

"You may have a brilliant academic record, Mr. Gray, but can you translate this into good teaching and staff management?" was Mr. Bronson's opening salvo.

Arthur was a bit unnerved by this approach. He knew that his success as a teacher would have been reported in the references which had been taken up on him before he was offered the interview for the job. Staff management? Well, this was an area in which Arthur would have to prove himself in post but, having already met the maths staff at Kelvinborough, he did not anticipate any major problem in that direction. Arthur knew he was a good organizer.

"The reputation of this school is built on its exam results," continued Mr. Bronson, "and I expect to see a considerable improvement in the results achieved by pupils in mathematics."

Arthur had seen the maths results for school when investigating Kelvinborough School as a potential post for himself and they hadn't seemed at all bad. Well, perhaps this was the sort of thing that head-teachers said to all newly appointed heads of department.

"I would suggest you have a word with Mr. Silvester," advised Mr. Bronson. "The results achieved in the chemistry department are the sort of results I would hope to see throughout the school. Mr. Silvester could give you some very good advice on how to get excellent exam results."

Arthur came away from that interview feeling somewhat unsettled. It struck him the Mr. Bronson would be a hard taskmaster without necessarily giving any encouragement to his staff.

Over the next few days, Arthur began to really get to know his fellow members of staff. He explained to the maths staff, the approach he had used in Bristol to motivate pupils to learn maths and they readily took this on board. Over the next few days, his staff came up with some ideas for really ingenious projects they'd thought up themselves to be used as teaching vehicles to meet the demands of the curriculum. Arthur was very impressed and felt encouraged by the fact that he obviously had an enthusiastic team working under him.

Inevitably, he encountered Mr. Silvester.

"Mr. Bronson asked me to have a word with you about getting the school maths exam results on track. They're nothing like as good as they should be." Mr. Silvester (Stinky) said in a challenging sort of way.

"Now I have contacts who could change all that but it will cost money!"

Arthur was really taken back by this approach.

"How much?"

"£300 in the first instance but, as your success grows, it could cost more."

"I assume the school pays for this service?" queried Arthur.

"Oh no, the scheme I work is a secret way by which teachers may do better than their colleagues, but it is a secret. Otherwise there would be nothing very special about it to enable teachers to outshine the competition. It works in favour of the individual members of staff who are ambitious for their own careers and who really want their pupils to be successful."

"Well, thank you, Mr. Silvester, but no. I'm quite confident that I can achieve good results without involving myself in expensive secret schemes."

Mr. Silvester looked quite put out by this response from someone he regarded as being very inexperienced.

"I think you are being very foolish, Mr. Gray. A young man like yourself at the beginning of his career could go really far, but without impressive exam results to enhance his reputation, he's going to remain at the bottom of the pile like most of the rest of the incompetents who masquerade as teachers at this school. If you want to reconsider your position, you know where to find me."

Stinky huffed and walked away.

Arthur immediately took a dislike to Stinky. He had learned that nick name when he overheard other teachers talking about the head of chemistry in a disparaging way.

A member of staff whom Arthur really took to was Ben Hardy, head of the physics department. They soon formed a close friendship. Mathematicians and physicists have a great deal in common and at the higher echelons of the profession, there is little to distinguish between them. Were Isaac Newton, James Clerk-Maxwell, Paul Dirac and Carl Gauss mathematicians or physicists?

Ben soon discovered that Arthur was a Christian and invited him along to St. Mark's church in Kelvinborough which he and his wife, Jane, attended.

Inevitably, Ben shared his opinions of other members of staff with Arthur. He didn't rate Mr. Bronson, the headmaster, very highly. It seems that this low rating was shared by most of the staff at Kelvinborough. However, the head didn't worry them very much. He hardly left his office and delegated tasks like taking assemblies and making returns to the Local Education Authority to his senior staff. The only time he made his presence felt in a serious way was when the exam results came out. He then emerged from his office to make disparaging comments about the school's performance. Even when the results were good by both local and national standards, Mr. Bronson was still critical. He continually pointed to the excellent chemistry results which represented the standard all departments should not only aim for but achieve.

This led to a sharing of views on Stinky. Arthur recounted both what Mr. Bronson had said about Mr. Silvester and the suggestion that Mr. Silvester had made to Arthur about the way to improve his department's exam results.

"You would do well to avoid Stinky and his suggestions," advised Ben. "Yes, he does get good exam results and we don't know how, but no-one here has been prepared to pay up front the sort of money that Stinky is demanding before he lets them in on his secret. It's almost as if he knows the exam questions in advance. I've discovered from my pupils that weeks before the exam, he sets his pupils mock exam papers whose questions cover in detail just the sections of the syllabus which feature in the actual exam paper. The questions he sets avoid being word for word exactly the same as the real exam but there's very little difference. No-one knows how Stinky does this and fortunately no-one has been prepared to get involved with what I imagine is Stinky's dirty secret. Exam board security is very tight so there's no way he could he could preview the exam papers."

Apart from the head and Stinky, there was no-one else about whom Ben had any negative comments except that he believed some of the staff who accompanied field trips adopted seriously unprofessional behaviour and that there were apparently attractive female members of staff whom he believed would exploit their charms to seduce male teachers! No names were mentioned because Ben had no proof that any of these misdemeanors he had recounted had actually taken place and therefore, he told Arthur not to quote him on what he'd just said. He admitted that in all probability, he was just sharing stories with Arthur which were no more than the malicious gossip which can spread like wildfire, in even the best of staff rooms. However, Ben had thought it best to warn Arthur that things in Kelvinborough School were not entirely as they should have been.

# Chapter 10

## The Failed Attempt at Seduction

Arthur had been at Kelvinborough School for about three weeks. He was really settling in very nicely. He'd already developed excellent relationships with his departmental staff who shared his enthusiasm to teach mathematics through the medium of projects which the pupils could recognize being relevant to real life. Passing their General Certificate of Secondary Education was no longer the sole objective of learning mathematics.

As he sat at his desk marking homework, he looked up as Georgina walked into the staff room. They hadn't met before because, when not teaching, Georgina spent most of her time in her office by one of the sports halls. The moment their eyes met, they both experienced a strange phenomenon. It was almost as if they had received a small electric shock, causing their hearts to miss a beat.

Ben, who was sitting nearby realized that because they taught different disciplines in a school with a large staff, Arthur and Georgina had not actually met and he introduced them. The thought had crossed Ben's mind that Georgina was a dangerous female predator from whom Arthur should be shielded but Georgina's reputation in this direction was no more than staff gossip. In any case, he realized that Arthur was a young, single man, well able to look after himself. From that time, Georgina's visits to the main staff room became much more frequent and a lot of that time was spent with Arthur.

Although it was only October, thoughts were already being given to organizing the staff children's Christmas party. To make a success of such an occasion, early preparation was necessary. It was always difficult to find a volunteer to take on this responsibility. Staff who had organized this event on previous occasions hadn't done a particularly good job and had come in for a lot of criticism from their fellow staff. Not unnaturally, they weren't prepared to undertake this again. Arthur reluctantly agreed to take this on this job on condition that those who'd done it before would share their experiences to acquaint Arthur with what was necessary and what were the pitfalls to avoid. Georgina readily volunteered to help Arthur with this task. This provided a pretext for Arthur and Georgina to meet to plan this event, both in and out of school hours. They soon developed a ready rapport.

Although a brunette rather than a blond, Arthur recognized that Georgina was every bit as pretty as Alice, but she was someone who had a wide general knowledge and could express her views well. World and national politics, sport, art, music, agriculture, horticulture, the environment, social issues, technology, history, you name it, Georgina had a sufficient depth of knowledge and well thought out opinions to more than hold her own in the lively discussions they often held. Having done well at her physics A-level, Georgina could even tax Arthur as they discussed matters relating to science, a subject which was very close to his own specialization. However, a topic they discussed more than anything was religion. Georgina took the stand of an atheist. Although she was nothing of the sort, a good discussion arose by her playing devil's advocate and coming at issues from the opposite direction that Arthur approached issues of faith.

Arthur and Georgina enjoyed going to the theatre and cinema together. They watched sporting events and made a point of supporting opposite teams when they went to a football match. Their relationship flourished until something happened which almost seriously jeopardized their friendship.

One evening, Arthur went round to Georgina's flat to make further arrangements for the party games and catering for the staff children's Christmas party. When he arrived, Arthur was surprised to find that Georgina was not dressed in the track suit she usually wore to lounge around in when off duty. She was bare-foot and wearing a silk dressing gown. When they had achieved the main planning objectives for the evening, Georgina went out into her kitchen to make coffee. When she returned, she had discarded the dressing gown and was wearing no more than a scanty bikini.

Arthur was alarmed.

"Why on earth are you dressed like that?" blurted out Arthur who was momentarily flustered.

"Because I'm very fond of you and I thought that would help us to get close together."

"But being in a state of undress like you are now with a young man in your flat is asking for trouble," Arthur said rather sharply.

"Well, I think I just might enjoy that sort of trouble," Georgina replied coyly.

Arthur realized that he was being paid a very great compliment but consensual sex was a path he didn't want to pursue. It went against the moral principles by which he'd always lived.

"Please put on your track suit and come back so we can just have coffee together," he said. "There's something very important I've been wanting to say to you for a long time."

Georgina went up to her bedroom and duly put on her track suit over her bikini. When she knew she was out of earshot she started to sob. Why had she been so foolish? Arthur would despise her. What a silly thing she'd done. It hadn't been like that when she'd just been dressed in the scanty kit she wore to teach some of her physical education classes when Ken had come to her office/changing room. The assertion that her former husband, Mike, had made, that all men were the same, just wasn't true.

It took some time for Georgina to compose herself sufficiently so that she felt she could face Arthur again. When she came back into the room, she found that Arthur was now sitting on the settee. He motioned for her to sit next to him.

"Georgina, I want you to know that you're the most beautiful, most intelligent young woman I've ever known. You must know that I love you very much but to have sex outside marriage would, for me, completely destroy our relationship." He continued, "But I've wanted to kiss you for a long time. May I kiss you now?"

Georgina leaned back into Arthur's arms and they enjoyed a long, lingering, passionate kiss. They sat back in silence for a few moments to recover their breath. Arthur felt bound to tell Georgina where he was coming from.

"You probably think me a frightful prude, believing that the only proper environment for sex is marriage. That attitude doesn't fit in with the modern day and age does it? Lots of folk may ask, 'what harm can come from two mature adults enjoying consensual sex together?' but I believe a lot of harm can come from it. Those who are affected in particular are children whose voice is just not heard on this subject. Their lives can so easily be tainted by the attitudes of their parents. This was specially brought home to me at my last school in Bristol. The school was in an affluent area of the city with no obvious social problems. But, oh, they were there, they were there in a very big and nasty way as I discovered from the English teacher.

She had asked a class of thirty eleven year olds to complete a series of sentences starting with the words,
"I wish..."

She expected to read sentences like "I wish I could have a new bike", "I wish I could go to Disney Land", "I wish I could have a dog".

Instead, twenty of the thirty pupils, that's two thirds of the class, made reference to domestic problems which obviously had their origin in sexual immorality. The sort of things they wrote were:-

> "I wish my father would return home!"
> "I wish my mother didn't have a boyfriend!"
> "I wish I had only one mum and dad so the other kids wouldn't make fun of me. I've three mums and three dads and they mess up my life!"
> "I wish my parents wouldn't fight all the time!"

Arthur paused and then continued,

"I hope to have only one sexual partner in life so that my children will grow up in such a secure family environment that worries arising from parental infidelity will never even have to cross their minds."

As Georgina listened to Arthur, she realized that Arthur's attitudes were exactly the same as her own had been before her disastrous marriage to Mike. Somehow, that marriage had degraded the high moral standards by which she had lived previously. She just hoped that Arthur would never find out about the way she had almost completely wrecked Ken's marriage and the impact that would have had on his children.

They sat in silence for a while, Georgina contemplating all that Arthur had just said to her. They finished their coffee and enjoyed another lingering kiss before Arthur left. They arranged to meet again, this time at Arthur's flat the following Thursday to put the final touches on the Christmas party plans.

After Arthur left, Georgina went upstairs and got ready for bed. Conflicting thoughts and emotions passed through her mind. Because she'd tried so crudely to seduce him, Arthur would now know her for the slut she was. A slut like her shouldn't be spending time with a decent young man like Arthur. Georgina cried for a bit. Then more pleasant thoughts crossed her mind. Arthur had said he loved her. She fell asleep, reliving the bliss of the wonderful kisses they had enjoyed together.

# Chapter 11

## The Failed Evangelist

After that fateful evening, the relationship between Arthur and Georgina didn't weaken but became even stronger. The children's Christmas party they'd jointly organized was a great success. They'd even persuaded Mr. Bronson to take on the role of Father Christmas and distribute the toys which Arthur and Georgina had chosen to be appropriate to the age and sex of each child attending. It had taken two complete evenings to get them all wrapped.

Arthur invited Georgina to attend church with him. Georgina had misgivings about this and they didn't arise because she was professing to Arthur that she was an atheist. No, Georgina thought that a woman like herself, (slut was the word that Mrs. Campbell had used in her tirade), shouldn't be sitting among all these virtuous people herself, making out that she too was a virtuous young woman. However, Arthur didn't know about her affair with Ken and she didn't want him to find out. In spite of feeling out of place in church, it was good to be seen with Arthur, to be enjoying his company and sharing his interests. Ben and his wife, Jane, too were happy to see Arthur and Georgina making such a handsome twosome. Whatever her reputation, Arthur couldn't do much better than to pair up with this attractive physical education teacher.

Georgina and Arthur had many discussions on religion and, coming from the stance of a professed atheist, this was one area where Georgina had difficulty in holding her own.

"If an alien were to land on earth on the Sahara desert and find a solar powered watch that someone had dropped in the sand and lost, what conclusions do you think the alien might come to?" Arthur challenged Georgina in one of their discussions.

"If he examined its workings and saw how it registered in a way which somehow kept up with the sun, he couldn't avoid coming to the conclusion that it had been made by an intelligent being," replied Georgina.

"Well," said Arthur, "how can you, who doesn't live in a desert but is surrounded by plant and animal life which is far more wonderful than the watch, fail to recognize that it has been put there by an intelligent being?"

Georgina didn't really have an answer for that.

"It's just the way atoms and molecules will develop and come together by natural processes without any external agency being involved," was her reply.

"Can the universe think then?" challenged Arthur.

"No, of course it can't!"

"How then do you think an unthinking universe was able to bring into existence human beings who can think and appreciate the universe, who can observe the most distant stars and wonder at them, human beings who can follow the ways atoms combine to form molecules? Can an unthinking universe spawn something greater than itself in its ability to think, to reason and to appreciate?"

"I can't answer, 'How?', but it has just happened through natural processes because of the properties of the atoms which make up the universe," was Georgina's rather weak answer to this challenge.

"God must have designed atoms from the beginning to have special properties which in due course would enable the fulfillment of his plans," answered Arthur. "Thus, the design of atoms can hardly be random. They have properties which even now, scientists can hardly understand, but which enable things to happen which are essential to the survival of life on earth as we know it."

"I'm not sure I follow that," queried Georgina. "Can you give me an example?"

"Take something as simple but as important as water," Arthur started to explain. "Nothing could survive without liquid water. Generally speaking, the lighter the molecule, the more likely it is to be a gas, but water, made up of almost the lightest molecules which exist, is not a gas but a liquid."

"Why should that be?" asked Georgina.

"The hydrogen atoms which combine with an oxygen atom to make a water molecule do not do so symmetrically but form what is called a dipole," explained Arthur. "This results in the molecules attracting one another quite strongly and they condense into a liquid at a much higher temperature than they would if this attraction did not exist."

"How amazing," responded Georgina.

"Yes," continued Arthur, "and that's not the end of it. Because of this dipole nature of the water molecules, a property of water called permittivity is amazingly high and this enables it to dissolve salts which other liquids like alcohol just can't! Because of this, water is an excellent cleaning agent."

"Yes, I think that I was taught something like that in my A-level physics at school," replied Georgina.

"Another truly amazing property of water," Arthur carried on explaining in his enthusiasm, "is that when water freezes into its solid state, ice, the solid is less dense than liquid water, resulting in ice forming at the surface of water rather than sinking to the bottom. In almost every other known substance, the solid form is denser than the liquid."

"Does this have any implications for life as we know it then?" challenged Georgina.

"Indeed it does," replied Arthur. "It means that in winter time, freshwater lakes and rivers freeze over at the top providing an insulating layer which allows the water beneath it to remain at a temperature of 4 degrees Celsius. This makes it possible for freshwater fish to survive the winter. If ice were denser than water, it would sink to the bottom as it is formed and in due course, the river or lake would just become solid ice in which no fish could survive."

"Is everything in nature that practical then?" queried Georgina.

"No, nature is also very beautiful," continued Arthur. "The dipole nature of water means that when water vapour freezes out into solid form, it generates the most beautiful six sided crystals like tiny, intricately designed jewels. We know these as snowflakes. No-one who has studied these crystals has ever discovered two which were identical!"

Georgina was amazed by all this and felt she needed to come up with her own challenge. "Evolution is a well-accepted scientific fact. However, it seems that to be a Christian, one has to accept that God made human beings quite separately from the evolutionary process. One can't accept that without committing intellectual suicide!"

"I know that many Christians, and indeed, some of the most sincere Christians I know, don't believe that man came about through evolution and they assert that they have to hold to this belief because that's what the Bible teaches," answered Arthur. "I think careful reading and interpretation of the Bible leads to a totally different conclusion."

"In what way?" asked Georgina.

"God has revealed himself to the human kind in remarkable ways. Two of the channels of this revelation are his Holy Word, the Bible, and science. Scientists have sometimes been defined as professionals who think God's thoughts after him. Now if we have a contradiction between two of the ways in which God reveals himself, we have a problem because God can't contradict himself. Although written at a time when it needed to be understood by primitive man who would have no concept of what is meant by an atom or a molecule or indeed, DNA, it is remarkable that sensible interpretation of the story tale language used in the book of Genesis in no wise contradicts the thinking of modern science. On the contrary, it actually supports it."

"Can you explain how the story of the creation of Adam converges with modern science then?" challenged Georgina.

"The word used by the Bible translators to represent the periods of time over which the stages of creation took place is rendered as 'a day'. However, the concept of a day has no meaning until you have a sun and an earth rotating on its axis as it orbits the sun. Therefore, it makes no sense to say the sun and the earth were created after a few days had elapsed. No, a sensible representation of the duration of each stage of creation would be a period of time which wasn't precisely specified," explained Arthur.

"We used to sing a hymn in school assemblies which went,

> 'A thousand ages in Thy sight
> Are as an evening gone,
> Short as the watch the ends the night
> Before the rising sun.' "

said Georgina, reinforcing Arthur's explanation of Biblical time.

Arthur continued, "The Bible states that God made man from the dust of the earth but it doesn't say how this process took place or indeed how long it took. It certainly doesn't say that God moulded man out of dust like one might make a plasticine model."

"How do you interpret the story of the creation of man?" asked Georgina.

"Evolution is a beautiful process, designed by God by which the dust of the earth can be formed over millions of years into living bodies including the body which has most of the attributes of man including his intelligence. However, that body was not a man but just an ape or a monkey. When the evolution of man reached that point, God did something very special. Quoting the Bible,

> 'And the Lord God formed man from the dust of the ground and breathed into his nostrils the breath of life; and the man became a living being.'

This breathing of God's Spirit into the creature God designed to be man is the crucial step in creating man who can enjoy fellowship with God. Every person has a small element of God's Spirit living within him or her, but by establishing the right relationship with God, that share of his Spirit may grow within a person. Many Christians have experienced baptism by the Holy Spirit by which they are so filled with

God's Spirit that they may perform supernatural acts."

"So it's the Spirit of God which he's breathed into man which makes him different and not his body or his intelligence?" said Georgina, following Arthur's argument.

"Yes, indeed," said Arthur. "It's not the body of a human which is important or even his brain. The body is no more than a temporary place for an element of God's Spirit to reside until the time comes to return this body back into the dust of the earth."

"Did evolution stop then, once man had been created?" asked Georgina.

"Certainly not, but God then introduced a new dimension into evolution." Arthur continued to explain. "It's undeniable that offspring share many of their parents' characteristics, their appearance, their intelligence, their strengths and weaknesses and this includes spiritual characteristics.

Every now and then, the offspring has qualities which although similar to, are superior to his or her parents. These are the offspring which evolution will tend to select to survive. Whereas, basic evolution proceeds to enable the survival of the fittest of creatures by natural selection, the Bible story shows how God has refined this process one step further and developed the human race by a process which we might call, spiritual selection."

"How does he do that?" asked Georgina, mystified but impressed by Arthur's closely knit argument.

"The Bible story shows how, of the descendants of Adam, only Noah was selected by God as a man with sufficient of his Spirit to further the human race. Of Noah's descendants, the spiritual selection occurred first through Shem, then through Abraham. Abraham's grandson, Jacob, was chosen in preference to his brother Esau by God to continue the process of spiritual selection and then, only through the tribes of Judah and Benjamin, to create a spiritual line of descent into which Jesus Christ could be born."

Arthur had obviously thought this out very well and Georgina had no answer to his carefully considered logic.

"Do you believe that Jesus existed?" Arthur challenged Georgina.

"Yes, I believe that," said Georgina. "His existence is the best attested fact of history but I don't believe that proves the existence of God, even though Jesus may have claimed to be the Son of God."

"It's said," continued Arthur, "that if Jesus hadn't really existed, it would have taken another Jesus, that is, someone equivalent to him in spiritual stature, to invent Jesus and write the gospels with their supreme moral teaching. There are only a few people one meets in life or reads about in history whose integrity of character is so great that one would be prepared to accept as authoritive, anything they said. Jesus is such a person. He demonstrated this authority, not just by his miracles and resurrection but by his quite remarkable and revolutionary teaching. If Jesus proclaimed that there is a God and he was God's son, that's good enough for me."

Once Arthur got going on his hobby horse, there was no stopping him.

"I've read of some recent research," continued Arthur, "carried out by scientists studying the way DNA develops. I wish I had kept a note of the source. From a knowledge of the molecules present and their concentration in the soup in which DNA is being developed, statisticians can work out the probability of molecules which will contribute to the formation of DNA coming together and combining on the basis that the movement of these molecules is completely random."

"This means then," challenged Georgina, seeing a possible weakness in Arthur's argument. "that creation is the result of random processes which is my contention."

"The great physicist, Einstein, said, 'God doesn't play dice!' " quoted Arthur. "This research by statisticians, which I have just mentioned, suggests that the processes are not entirely random and this may mean that the hand of God is directing it. From knowing the probability that molecules involved in the formation of DNA will come together to combine in the process of building even more complex molecules, the statisticians can work out the frequency of such events. This in turn, enables them to deduce how quickly DNA molecules will develop. It turns out that in fact, the DNA molecules form much, much more rapidly than the statisticians' predictions. Hence, the movement of these molecules can't be completely random. A possible explanation of why this is so lies in recognizing that God is in control of the process of creation and can intervene to accelerate the development of DNA in line with his purposes."

While she would not admit it because she enjoyed the cut and thrust of debate with Arthur, Arthur had convinced Georgina that his beliefs were sound and valid, that there was indeed a God.

It was a pity that Arthur just relied on intellectual arguments to prove the existence of God to Georgina, and hadn't done more to present the character of Jesus as the only Son of God and Saviour of mankind.

It was a pity that Georgina continued with the pretence that she was an atheist, even though she'd been convinced by Arthur's arguments. Their discussions on religion had hardly featured Jesus and therefore, Georgina hadn't been brought to recognize Jesus as one who loved her more than she could imagine and who'd died to save her.

It was clear to everyone around that Arthur and Georgina were meant for each other, but because they'd approached the theological discussions they'd had with each other from opposite standpoints, an unbridged chasm lay between them. In due course, this would lead to future sadness.

# Chapter 12

## The Indian City

Arthur considered that he'd a vocation to serve his church by using his skills to work in a developing country. As he'd realized when he was going out with Alice, he knew that it would be unfair to ask a woman who didn't share his faith at a deep level to accompany him to work in an inhospitable climate, however much he loved her and she loved him. He felt that Georgina would feel unhappy and out of place in a third world country. He hadn't yet met the young woman who would share his Christian faith so that he and she could jointly serve God and their church. This was an ideal that his Cambridge friends, Paul and Helen, had realized.

Then, one day, as Arthur was browsing through the church magazine, his attention was drawn to an advert expressing the need for teachers to work in India, Kenya or Sri Lanka. They would work under the patronage of a missionary society which went by the name, 'Gift of the Gospel'. Arthur applied and was accepted with open arms. There was a school in Mumbai (Bombay) which seemed to be just right for Arthur. There'd be no need for him to learn a new language. English was the lingua franca in Mumbai, especially so, as this bridged the gap between sections of the community which spoke different languages including Hindi, Gujarati and Marathi. Arthur would teach in English but he might find it helpful in getting alongside the population if he learnt one of the native languages as well.

Several months would elapse before he could be granted a visa and work permit by the Indian government but there were a series of preparatory steps which Arthur had to take himself before he could embark on this new phase of his life. He had to have inoculations against a number of tropical diseases. He had to work out his notice at Kelvinborough School. Most difficult of all, he had to break the news to Georgina that he'd be continuing his career in India.

Of course, Georgina was upset by Arthur's decision to take this step, almost to the extent of being distraught. Hadn't Arthur told her that he loved her? What did that mean now? Georgina was now an emotionally stable, mature woman. She didn't react in the same way that she'd done when her relationship with Jacob foundered during the time that she was an undergraduate. In reality, she never expected to be more than a good friend to Arthur. She'd erroneously considered him to be too good and too clever for her. Life would have to go on without Arthur.

Arthur promised that he would send Georgina his address when he knew just where he would be living but this wouldn't become clear until he was actually in Mumbai.

Arthur arrived in India in the middle of September, just as the monsoon season was coming to an end. He took a fortnight to acclimatize himself, before he embarked on teaching at the school of 'St. Thomas'.

Although very different from England, one aspect of Mumbai helped Arthur to feel at home in this city and that was the architecture of so many of the important buildings. Mumbai has been described as one of the most characteristically Victorian cities in the world. This description owes itself to the fact that so many of these buildings had gone up during the time of the Raj in a style which has been described as Mumbai Gothic. This was a blend of Victorian Gothic with contemporary local styles. Perhaps the most famous of these buildings is the Gateway of India, so called, because this would be the first building Europeans encountered as they entered India via the port of Mumbai. The University of Mumbai with its Rabaji Tower, modelled on Big Ben, the Mumbai City Hall and Chhatrapi Shivaji Terminus all demonstrate Victorian influence.

When Arthur started his work in the school, he found Indian children were a pleasure to teach. He made friends with both the local people and the expatriate population who attended the Anglican church in that part of Mumbai. The young Indian women were both beautiful and charming but Arthur found developing relationships with them was difficult because they would never express an opinion which was in any way different to his own. In some ways, they were a bit like the Alice he had known in Cambridge. Arthur felt the reluctance of these ladies to get involved in any sort of controversy with a man was a cultural thing in that male dominated society rather than that they didn't have opinions of their own.

Arthur attempted to learn Hindi but this was an uphill task. The script was so different from the Latin letters used to write English. Without a fluent knowledge of a native language, Arthur felt his capacity to serve his sponsors, 'Gift of the Gospel', as a missionary was very limited. Arthur made some progress in Hindi when he arranged with one of his church friends to spend a few hours each week with him, learning conversational skills in the language.

Mumbai is almost choked by the most congested traffic in the world. Arthur was initially somewhat disturbed by the morass of crowded streets with the monotonous, unmusical moan of poorly maintained motors conducting melancholic motorists who miserably meandered through this metropolitan maze competing to make meaningful movement towards modest objectives in the minimum time. Mumbai, more than most cities, needs to proceed with the demolition of buildings which obstruct the creation of an efficient street plan. However, vested interests in the form of the owners of property just prevent this happening. Indeed, few cities have managed to keep their road systems abreast of the exponentially increasing demands of traffic. London had such an opportunity after the Great Fire of 1666 but property owners had reclaimed the patches of ground where their shops had been while the charred ruins were still smoking, obstructing the imposition of a rationalized London street plan. Paris is exceptional in that Baron Haussmann was able to remodel the street plan of the city over the period of the Second Empire during the nineteenth century to create the magnificent tree lined boulevards for which the City is so famous.

However, traffic congestion hasn't prevented Mumbai from becoming extremely wealthy. Indeed, Mumbai is the wealthiest city in India. It comes in the top ten globally for the number of billionaires living there.

Arthur contributed well to the work of both the school and the church. As in England, his method of teaching maths was efficient and aroused enthusiasm among his pupils. However, it was important to Arthur that his work should have a spiritual dimension. It was discovered that he was an eloquent preacher and he was invited to deliver sermons in church and to take assemblies at school. He started a midweek discussion group which dealt with questions which Arthur felt were relevant to people living in that culture, by considering topics such as :-

How is my gender best used in the service of God?

> *Arthur felt a discussion based on this question could expose aspects of a male dominated society and help women to discover how special they were.*

What distinguished the classes of people living in India and are these distinctions in line with God' purposes?

> *Arthur was particularly disturbed to find that, although illegal, discrimination still existed against a class known as Daljits (formerly referred to as untouchables) even by churchgoers!*

Should the priorities of a democratically governed country be more concerned with relieving poverty than in developing weapons?

> *Arthur had posed this question because he was disturbed that India had spent vast resources in developing its own atomic bomb while the issue of relieving the extreme poverty in some of its cities remained unaddressed. The development of atomic weapons by India and Pakistan over border disputes in the Kashmir region was no more than expensive sabre rattling. There was no conceivable scenario where these weapons could have been used.*

These discussion groups were well attended and Arthur was encouraged to find that the ladies present had found their tongues and could present well-reasoned arguments to express their opinions. Arthur ran these groups in such a way that the people attending reached their conclusions through their own contributions to the discussion without Arthur having to politically compromise himself by expressing his views. He usually found that at the end of a discussion meeting, the prevailing point of view was very much in line with his own point of view anyway.

# **Chapter 13**

## **The Shining Haven**

Although Arthur was contributing so well to the work of the school and the church, he confided with the school head-teacher, Surinder Matthu, that he felt dissatisfied that he wasn't doing much to help ordinary Indian people who didn't attend church. He felt that this was very much due to his limited fluency in Hindi.

Surinder arranged for Arthur to meet an English expatriate, Jennifer Hurst. Jennifer was a plump women in her mid-forties who had the happiest disposition that Arthur had ever encountered in any person. Jennifer took Arthur to see the work in which she was involved.

Like all other large cities, Mumbai has its slums and population problems although the extent of the poverty is nothing like as bad as in other large Indian cities like Kolkata (Calcutta). Some of Mumbai's problems in this direction are related to the collapse of the textile industry in the 1970's. Jennifer Hurst had worked for some years in one of these areas among the street children, providing them with food, shelter and a rudimentary education, from a centre called 'the Shining Haven'. She was supported by a dedicated team of Indian helpers and received limited funds from a generous group of friends in England. Most of the children at the Shining Haven were either orphans or had been abandoned at a young age by irresponsible parents. Some had homes to go to but their parents were desperately poor and they preferred their children to spend their time at the Shining Haven during the day, rather than grubbing around the city's rubbish heaps in the hope of finding items of sufficient value to be worth retrieving.

Arthur discovered that he could contribute to this work during the time he wasn't teaching in 'St. Thomas School'. Although he couldn't be at the Shining Haven much during the working day and hence, was unable to contribute to the very rudimentary education being provided there, he could do a lot about repairing the accommodation at the Shining Haven during out of school hours. It was in a really ramshackle state. Although an academic, Arthur had good carpentry skills. With wood and tools he supplied at his own expense, he set about mending broken door and window frames, replacing rotten floorboards and repairing the roof at no small risk to himself.

On Saturday afternoons, assisted by one of Jennifer's Indian helpers, Arthur organized games for these children on a patch of rough open land near the Shining Haven. Again, Arthur supplied the recreational equipment, balls, bats, netball hoops, at his own expense but his generosity was more than repaid by seeing the joy these children, from a grossly underprivileged background, exhibited as they participated in the fun of properly organized games.

Arthur then experienced a misfortune. One morning, he woke up feeling cold. He started to shiver and developed a headache which was so intense that he couldn't go to school. He felt very fatigued. Manjit Parshottam, the lady from whom he rented his room, called the doctor. By the time the doctor arrived, Arthur was sweating profusely. The doctor took Arthur's temperature. As expected, it was severely raised.

"You have a classic case of malaria," Arthur was advised. "You'll need to rest up for a couple of days but it'll soon pass off. I'll prescribe some medicine for you which will ease the symptoms."

Although Arthur had had his inoculations before coming to India, there's no vaccine which provides protection from malaria. When he left England, Arthur's doctor had prescribed for him anti-malaria tablets and insect repellant to rub on his skin. Also, Arthur slept under a mosquito net. However, he'd been a bit careless recently about taking his tablets and the inevitable had happened. He was bitten by an infected mosquito.

True to the doctor's word, Arthur felt much better after three days and was able to return to his work at 'St. Thomas School' and was also able to continue his support of the Shining Haven.

From that time onwards, Arthur was much more careful about taking his anti-malaria tablets and using insect repellent. However, no precautions are completely foolproof against malaria. Arthur had another bout three months later. As before, rest and medication led to a good recovery.

Arthur enjoyed good health for another six months and then malaria struck again. This time the symptoms were much more serious. In addition to the raised temperature, headaches and sweat, Arthur started to vomit. He also experienced breathing problems.

The doctor was very grave when he pronounced his prognosis.

"I fear that you may have contracted the most severe form of malaria. It's caused by a parasite called plasmodium falciparum. I think that you'll recover this time but this illness can be accompanied by organ failure which could be fatal. I strongly advise you to return home to England. Unfortunately, malaria hangs round in the system. Bouts of malaria symptoms will recur from time to time, even when you are in England, but they won't be anything as acute as those you are experiencing now."

What was Arthur to do now?

# Chapter 14

## The Successful Evangelist

Life wasn't the same for Georgina after Arthur had left for India. She felt no man could replace Arthur as a companion but her friendship intensified with another member of staff with whom she got on extremely well. Kathleen joined the school soon after Georgina had been appointed to the physical education section and they soon formed a firm friendship.

Kathleen Morrison was the technician in the chemistry department. She was a graduate of Kelsover University. Kelsover University had started as a Technical College, but had experienced a rapid series of upgrades, first to become a Polytechnic, then a College of Advanced Technology (CAT), and finally, was awarded university status. Work in school laboratories was becoming so technical that someone like Kathleen of graduate status was needed to cope with the many demands made on the technician's skill.

There is no doubt that Kathleen was a very capable young woman but Stinky Silvester, her line manager, was disparaging about her qualifications. He didn't rate the City and Guilds Advanced Certificate she had earned before going to university and frequently stated that a degree awarded from a jumped up CAT wasn't worth the paper it was written on.

Georgina had taken a dislike to Stinky from the time she joined the school and she frequently found herself commiserating with Kathleen over the inconsiderate behaviour of her boss and the rudeness with which he spoke to her in front of others.

Georgina told Kathleen that now Arthur had moved on, she no longer felt like going to St. Mark's church without him. Kathleen went to St. Peter's church in a different part of Kelvinborough and she suggested that

Georgina should come to church with her there.

"I shouldn't really be going to church at all," confessed Georgina. "I've done some wrong things in my life which I'm really ashamed of now and I don't feel it's right for me to come to church and sit among virtuous people as if I was really one of them myself. I'm no more than a disgusting slut."

"Do you really think that the only people who go to church are good?" countered Kathleen. "Church isn't a club for saints but a school for sinners. In my teens I was the nastiest, cattiest, rudest, most ungrateful girl you could imagine."

"I can't believe you were ever like that," said Georgina incredulously. "You are one of the sweetest, most gentle people I know."

"I'm afraid I was," continued Kathleen. "I wasn't happy. I knew that I was a nasty bit of goods but I didn't seem to be able to do anything about it."

"How did you become like you are now then?" queried Georgina.

Kathleen explained, "A friend took me to church and I realized from what the minister said that I could change my life if I was prepared to dedicate it to the Christ who had died to take my sins upon himself. Well, I made that decision. I prayed and acknowledged to Jesus that I was a nasty person who desperately wanted to turn her life around. I told him that I knew he had died to take people's sins upon himself, and promised that if he would take my sins away, I would live only for him."

"Did that make a difference?" asked Georgina, thinking that what Kathleen had told her sounded just too easy a way to turn around one's life.

"Indeed, it did," continued Kathleen. "It happened, just like that. When I stood up from my prayer, I felt a different person. I told my friend what I'd done and she said I can see the change in you already. And yes,

I had changed. I began to read the Bible every day and I prayed to Jesus and I found I no longer wanted to be rude or say nasty things. I just wanted to serve Jesus. I had given my life to Jesus, so whenever I wasn't sure about what to say or do when a decision was called for, I found myself asking myself, 'What would Jesus do?' "

"Well, I can see that you're a lovely person now," commented Georgina. "but I can't imagine you ever being any different."

"Well, I certainly was," asserted Kathleen. "I realise now how unhappy and miserable I was before I made that commitment, but everything has been different since. I can't describe the joy I have felt since I asked Jesus to control my life. I can even put up with Stinky's rudeness without feeling any resentment."

Kathleen then turned her attention to Georgina.

"I can't think what you have to feel ashamed about, Georgina. You seem such a totally nice person but I know that all of us, even the best of us, have sin which only Jesus can take away. We can then fully enjoy the life that comes from serving him."

So it was that Georgina went to St. Peter's church with Kathleen. It was a special evangelistic service. Georgina enjoyed the hushed atmosphere amid the gothic beauty of that building as she sat quietly there before the service started. She felt uplifted by the hymn singing and the minister's address was really inspiring. When the minister invited those who hadn't already done so to make a commitment to Christ, Georgina felt she had to make the same commitment that Kathleen had made. Later in the service, the minister invited all those who wanted to make such a commitment to come to the front where they could talk about this to a counsellor. Kathleen accompanied Georgina to the front of the church and left her there as the minister prayed for the half dozen or so people who had come forward to make a commitment to Jesus. At the end of this prayer, individual counsellors came and met each person who'd come to the front. They then went as couples to different quiet areas in the church or to the rooms leading off the main church building.

Georgina had been met by a lady called Joan. Georgina may have classified Joan as middle aged but she was probably no more than forty-five, if that. Georgina told Joan about her failed marriage, of how she'd seduced a married man with children and almost caused his wife to divorce him. She confessed that although she knew she had done wrong, even after that, she'd tried to seduce a young man whom she admired very much.

"Can Jesus really forgive sins like that?" she asked Joan.

"Jesus can and does forgive even worse sins than that for anyone who admits their sin and really wants to change their life, and there's no doubt in my mind that you're such a person."

Georgina told Joan that she wanted to commit her life to Jesus.

Joan asked Georgina about her friends and was very reassured when Georgina told her about Kathleen. Joan knew Kathleen well and realized that she would give Georgina good support in her new found Christian faith.

After Joan had prayed for Georgina, she conducted her back into the main part of the church which was now empty but for a few people waiting for friends being counselled. Kathleen was waiting for Georgina and Georgina declared that she now felt the same sort of joy that Kathleen had told her about when she'd asked Georgina to come to church.

"When you next go to church and look around at the people there," said Kathleen, "don't think of them as specially good people in whose company you are out of place. They're all sinners like you and me, but they've done what you've just done tonight and dedicated their lives to Jesus."

After that service, Georgina and Kathleen grew even closer. Kathleen encouraged Georgina to study the Bible. Georgina joined the home group which Kathleen belonged to. This met weekly for prayer and Bible study. The group was mixed in age, intellect and gender but this was no problem for Georgina. She did so value the time she spent with them and learnt so much from what they could teach her.

# Chapter 15

## Cyber Crime

One day, Kathleen came to Georgina to tell her about a discovery she'd made which created a problem she didn't know how to deal with.

"One of the jobs I do for the Chemistry department is to file all their paper work. This includes the exam papers which the pupils sit." she told Georgina. "Well, something strange struck me about the internal mock exam papers which the department sets just before A-levels and GCSE's. Although the actual wording may be different, the questions are the same as those in the actual exam papers set by the exam board. I thought that Stinky can't possibly know the questions in advance because the actual exam papers are opened from sealed envelopes in front of the candidates on the day they sit their exam.

Anyway, I did a bit of detective work. I can easily hack into Stinky's e-mail because I know where he hides his password. When I did so, I found a set of e-mails sent from someone under the name, 'examfacilitator@qmail.com'. When I looked through these e-mails, I found that they were the GCSE and A-level papers set for the past few years, but the e-mails were dated before the actual exam dates. Exam boards don't usually, no, they never send out exam papers in advance of the actual exams in this way.

What should I do? I can't tell Stinky. For a start, he'd get me sacked for hacking into his e-mail."

Georgina thought for a minute. This revelation was not actually a surprise to her. Arthur had told her about the suggestion Stinky had made to him soon after he joined the school and it was a mystery to other staff how Stinky could set test papers in advance of the real exams whose questions so closely resembled the exam papers when they came out.

"Should I tell the head?" continued Kathleen.

Normally, this would have been the best thing to have done but Georgina just didn't trust the head. Also, Stinky was the only member of staff who had a close relationship with Mr. Bronson.

"No," advised Georgina. "I don't trust Mr. Bronson. He may already know about Stinky's scheme but goes along with it because he knows that it achieves good exam results for the school. The very fact he advises staff to go to Stinky to get advice on improving their exam results points in this direction.

Give me a set of the mock exam questions Stinky has set over the last few years. They shouldn't be considered 'confidential documents', once these exams have been taken. I'll send them to the chief examiner at the exam board and see what his reaction might be. I'll explain that these questions have been set in the chemistry department before the actual GCSE and A-level exams take place. I'll also ask him why the actual exam papers are sent from the e-mail address, 'examfacilitator@qmail.com' before the date of the real exam.

I'll explain that I am sticking my neck out because I'm only a junior member of staff at Kelvinborough School but am acting on my own initiative because there's no one more senior at the school whom I can trust to deal with this. I'll ask the chief examiner therefore to keep my name strictly confidential because I could face dire consequences if it becomes known in some quarters that I've written to him.

If this backfires, the buck will stop with me and there is no reason for anyone to know of your discovery or involvement, Kathleen."

"Would you really do this Georgina? I feel you are taking a frightful risk."

"Somewhere, I've learnt at one of our Bible study meetings that a definition of sin is 'knowing the right thing to do and not doing it'. Yes I'll certainly communicate with the exam board but I think we should pray about this first."

Georgina and Kathleen prayed earnestly for a good half hour. At the end of their time of prayer, they both felt strongly convinced that although risky, Georgina had suggested the right course of action.

When the chief examiner received Georgina's letter, he was most alarmed. This breach of security reflected very badly on the exam board and if it came to light, it might even result in the board losing its licence. The board's computer experts were set the task of finding the source of this breach. It didn't prove too difficult for them. They discovered the culprit. He was Jack Smith, a junior technician. When confronted, Jack had no alternative but to acknowledge that he'd nosed around places he shouldn't have been and discovered the passwords which enabled him to access the exam papers. These he'd sent in advance to Mr. Silvester at Kelvinborough School and received payment for his services.

Jack Smith was sacked of course but he was further warned that if he made any further communication with Mr. Silvester, criminal proceedings would be taken against him, and they assured Jack they would know if any such communication occurred. The reason the board had not prosecuted Jack on this occasion was its fear of the negative repercussions and worse that would arise if such a serious failure in the security of the board became public knowledge and got reported in the press. They didn't make this fact known to the sacked employee as a reason for their apparent lenience. Taking overt action against Mr. Silvester also carried the risk of adverse publicity for the board. The board worked out another strategy to deal with Mr. Silvester.

The chief examiner phoned Georgina and asked her to phone him back on a private line. (This was a communication of which the board didn't want a hard copy record.) The chief examiner expressed the board's most sincere and deep gratitude for drawing their attention to this serious breach in their security which they described as cyber crime. He asked Georgina how they could reward her, pointing out that because of the repercussions of any publicity associated with this event, they were limited in the action they could take and they did not want to jeopardise her career. They assured her however, that the board employee who'd committed this crime had been sacked and they were preparing to take appropriate action against Mr. Silvester.

Georgina assured the board that she'd only done what she considered to be her duty and wanted no reward.

The board arranged to send Mr. Silvester a set of exam papers which consisted of questions quite different from the ones which were actually set for the real exam from the e-mail address, 'examfacilitator@qmail.com'

The impact of this stratagem was not felt until the day of the examination. Stinky went down to see his students settled for the exam. The papers were distributed and Stinky casually glanced at the questions. The second glance was not casual. The invigilators present were unaware of what the exam board had done and were alarmed to see Stinky turn pink and then almost purple with rage. He strode out of the examination hall in an obviously foul frame of mind. He spent most of the rest of the morning, ensconced with Mr. Bronson who was almost certainly in on the dishonest practice in which his head of chemistry had been involved.

When the exam results came out later that summer, everyone except Stinky and Mr. Bronson was surprised but secretly delighted to see that the chemistry results were absolutely abysmal.

# Chapter 16

## A Courageous Act

Georgina was returning to the main staffroom after her first class of the morning in the smaller of the two sports halls. She heard what sounded like a shot. The staffroom door was suddenly flung open and teachers rushed out in a mad stampede.

"Take cover, Georgina," someone yelled. "Aslam Akram's in there with a gun. He's just shot Stinky!"

Georgina knew Aslam. He was a very pleasant inoffensive boy. She'd taught his class history last term, during one of the time-table slots when she was not down to be in the sports hall. Georgina wasn't the sort of person who panicked. In spite of the warning she'd been given, she carried on past staff rushing in the opposite direction and entered the staff room.

The first thing she noticed was Stinky, slumped on the floor, bleeding fairly profusely. She looked up and not far away was Aslam, nervously standing there, holding a gun pointing at his own head. She felt Stinky's pulse. No, he wasn't dead but he was in desperate need of first aid.

"Wait there, Aslam," she commanded in a surprisingly calm voice. "I'll just get Mr. Silvester out of here and then I'll come back so that we can have a chat."

Georgina dragged Stinky through the door by his shoulders and yelled out to the staff who were anxiously peering round the doors of nearby rooms,
"This man needs first aid!   Call an ambulance quickly!"

The emergency services had in fact already been alerted and were on their way to Kelvinborough School.

Georgina re-entered the staff room and closed the door behind her. Aslam was still standing there, twitching as he held the gun to his head.

"Don't be silly, Aslam. Put the gun down, it might go off," she said quietly. "Come and sit here and tell me why you shot Mr. Silvester."

She sat down and gestured to a chair opposite her. Aslam sat down. He no longer pointed the gun at his head but still held it. "Why did you shoot Mr. Silvester?"

"He said that the birth of Mohammed was the worst calamity which had ever occurred in human history."

The fact that Stinky had had a politically incorrect outburst did not surprise Georgina. This was just typical of the man.

"I told the Imam Khatib at my mosque and he told me that I should go and shoot Mr. Silvester and then shoot myself. I would then go immediately to Jannah. There I would be happy and have everything I long for, good food, lovely clothes."

"Where did you get the gun?"

"The Imam drove me to a secret house and spoke to a man I'd never seen before who gave me a box which contained this gun. I was told it was loaded with two shots, one for Mr. Silvester and one for myself."

"Did you believe your Imam?"

"He said he was telling me what it said in the Koran. Every Muslim has to believe the Koran."

"Have you read the Koran yourself?"

"I've tried to. I've been to a Madrasa to learn how to do it. We're supposed to read it in Arabic but I find Arabic very difficult so I rely on what the Imam's tell me."

Looking over Aslam's shoulder through the staffroom window, Georgina could see that a lot of activity was going on outside. Two police cars had arrived with sirens blaring and parked on the playground. Men dressed in black and carrying rifles had climbed on to the roof of the classroom block, opposite the staffroom. Suddenly, a voice was heard from a loud hailer.

"We have every door and window covered. Put the gun down and come out with your hands up!"

"They're police marksmen," explained Georgina to Aslam. "They've got guns because they think you're going to shoot someone else. Let's change places so that I can sit between you and the window. Then, if they're silly enough to shoot, they'll hit me before they shoot you."

As they changed places, Georgina saw a black police car arrive on the playground and the officer who got out looked to be a very senior person.

"Do you think Mohammed really minds if people say silly things about him. There are so many more important things going on on earth for him and Allah to pay attention to. Allah, or God as we call him, is a big God who's been there for a long time. He's not going to be affected much by someone like Mr. Silvester saying something inappropriate. He'll deal with little people like Mr. Silvester who say silly things, after death. We'll all be judged by God after we have died. Far better to let Allah deal with this sort of problem then than try to deal with it ourselves now.

Allah has given you a life to live, Aslam. What do you think he wants to do with it?"

Aslam thought for a moment in silence.

Just then, the staffroom telephone rang.

"Sit still, Aslam. I'll deal with it."

Georgina went to the telephone on the next desk and picked it up.

"Georgina speaking."

"Miss Matthews, this is Superintendent Grice here, Head of the Anti-terrorism Unit. Can you appraise us of the situation? Is it safe to send in a police negotiator?"

"Everything is under control. I am carrying on with negotiations very well myself. At present, I don't need support from police negotiators. I hope that we will come out in a minute. Would you tell your police marksmen to stand down and the man with the loud hailer not to broadcast any more silly messages."

"Leave the phone off the hook and keep us in touch with any development," the Superintendent instructed.

Georgina put the phone down on the desk and returned to Aslam. Georgina was glad that the police would be able to hear her as she continued to talk to Aslam. Aslam hadn't answered her last question.

"Don't you think it's wrong of imams to ask young people like yourself to do something which will end their lives when they could very easily do what they are asking themselves? You've got your life ahead of you. You could do a wonderful job, perhaps become a doctor or paramedic which would really be helpful to people. You could hopefully get married."

Aslam realized that Miss Matthews was talking a lot of sense. He felt he could trust this teacher far more than he could his imam.

Georgina continued, "You've seen how Muslim suicide bombers have killed hundreds of innocent people all over the world, not just in this country but in America, in Turkey, in France, in Pakistan. Do you really think that Allah wants to kill hundreds of innocent people, including many good Muslims, just because some imam says so? The bomb which killed hundreds of people in Turkey was being carried by someone younger than you are,

Aslam. He won't be able to live a life and do good things to please Allah like you'll be able to do."

"That's all I've ever wanted to do," said Aslam, almost in a sob. "I've relied on the imams to tell me what that is. My imam told me to shoot Mr. Silvester."

Georgina realized that she could discredit Aslam's imam.

"Did you know that in the Koran, Mohammed teaches that it's wrong for a person to take up arms against a country which has given him shelter, and yet, that's what some imams are asking young Muslims like yourself to do?

Come on, Aslam. Put the gun down on the table and we'll go out."

Aslam realized the seriousness of his predicament and the likely consequences. "I'm going to be in trouble."

"Yes, you are, but the good thing is that you're still alive with a life ahead of you in which you'll be able to please Allah by doing things to help other people rather than killing them. Come on Aslam. Put that gun down."

Aslam rested the gun on the table in front of him. Georgina picked up the phone.

"Superintendent Grice, Aslam has put down the gun. We're unarmed. We're ready to come out now."

Georgina put the phone down.

"Come with me," Georgina said to Aslam.

Aslam sighed and nervously picked himself up.

They stood and walked out of the room, leaving the gun on the table. A team of police officers were waiting outside. One of them rushed into the staffroom to recover the gun. Aslam was taken off into some sort of custody. It all happened very quickly. A senior officer came up to Georgina. This was Superintendent Grice. He shook Georgina's hand.

"Thank you Miss Matthews. You've done well, really well."

By this time, school staff had come out of their refuges and appeared on the scene. They surrounded Georgina, hugging her and showering her with plaudits. Even Mr. Bronson who had made a rare excursion from his office due to the emergency came and thanked Georgina.

He said, "Drop into my office, when you can, Miss Matthews. We'll see if we can work out a way to properly celebrate the wonderful job you've done this morning."

Stinky made a good recovery and was soon back at school but he decided to resign from teaching at the end of the term. He no longer lived in the aura of being the teacher whose pupils always got the best exam results.

Aslam had to serve a term in youth custody. Technically, he was a minor and in passing sentence, the judge took account of the pressure to which Aslam had been subjected by his religious leader.

His imam was convicted of being a preacher of hate and was dealt with much more severely.

# Chapter 17

## A wedding

Arthur was settling into a new school in the Home Counties. He was sad to have had to leave India but the doctor had not hidden the serious risk to his health that he would face if he remained in that inhospitable climate. Malaria affects so many in India but Arthur had been unfortunate enough to contract a potentially fatal version of the disease.

"If God had wanted me to work in India," thought Arthur, "why didn't he protect me from this disease?"

It's very easy for a person to superimpose what they themselves believe God wants them to do on God's actual plan for their lives. A person's preconceived ideas may be entirely different from God's purpose. Arthur hadn't done the wrong thing in going to India in response to what he believed God's plan for him might be.

Indeed, he had done the right thing in trying the door. He had tried the door but to his surprise, God had closed it for him. If God does this, it usually means that he has other plans for the person concerned. Perhaps, by allowing Arthur to go away for a bit, he'd been able to bring other things about which were necessary for the fulfilment of his master plan.

As Arthur and Georgina looked back on this period of their lives and considered the mistakes they had made which could have ruined their lives, but which, in a strange way, had been resolved to give rise to a very happy outcome, they often used to say to each other,

'God works in a mysterious way, his wonders to perform.'

Arthur had had a quick meal at the local café after school had ended and he now returned home to relax. He settled into the armchair and picked up the paper.

Sensational headlines were spread across the front page.

## *Brave teacher thwarts gun toting schoolboy terrorist.*

As he browsed through the article, he suddenly sat up when he discovered the school in question was Kelvinborough. His attention became even more focused when he discovered that the brave teacher was none other than Georgina. He carried on reading.

> *On being asked why she was prepared to go into a staff room where she knew there was a pupil with a gun who was prepared to use it, Miss Georgina Matthews (24) replied, "I knew there was an injured colleague in that room who was perhaps in danger of dying. As someone who's recently become a Christian, I had no alternative but to see if I could possibly help him."*

Arthur could barely reconcile this with what he knew of Georgina, the young woman he had loved but whose atheism had acted as a barrier between them. Here she was, proclaiming she'd become a Christian!

Arthur's time table enabled him to finish early the following day and he immediately drove the fifty or so miles to Kelvinborough. He drove into the school car park and had no difficulty in identifying Georgina's Ford Ka. He parked his car nearby and waited for Georgina to come out. She was one of the last to leave and as she made her way to her car, Arthur got out of his and stood up. Georgina paused as she saw Arthur, hardly believing her eyes. Then she rushed into Arthur's arms and burst into tears. Arthur felt tears running down his cheeks too.

"Why didn't you write?" was a question they almost simultaneously asked each other.

Barely a day went by when Georgina didn't think of Arthur, and Georgina had never been far from Arthur's thoughts.

They realized that they had a lot of catching up to do.

"Let's grab a meal at the White Lion," said Arthur. "We must have so much news to share. I really want to hear how you managed to foil that schoolboy terrorist."

They talked and talked till closing time. Yes, Arthur had written giving Georgina his Mumbai address. The letter had never reached her. One is inclined to put this down to the inefficiency of the Indian postal service but the British postal service is not infallible. Neither of them had bothered with social media, facebook or twitter, and as they'd never had occasion to e-mail each other, they didn't know their e-mail addresses. Sadly, this had meant that a year had passed without their being able to communicate and a lot had happened in that year.

Arthur told Georgina about the school of St. Thomas where he had worked, the church he had attended in India, his work among the street children at the Shining Haven and the malaria which was the cause of his having to leave India.

Georgina told Arthur how her friendship with Kathleen had blossomed, of how they had exposed Stinky's exam paper scam, and very specially, of her conversion at St. Peter's Church.

Over the next few weeks, Arthur and Georgina made up for the time they might have spent together but for Arthur being in India. Georgina took Arthur to meet her parents who soon developed a great affection for this intelligent and charming young man.

As they spent time together and their love for each other deepened, Arthur and Georgina realized that they could not live apart. One evening, Arthur went down on one knee and asked Georgina if she would marry him.

"Of course," she said. "I thought you were never going to ask."

Greg and Julie Matthews were delighted when they heard the news. Arthur fitted the image of the sort of man they wanted their daughter to marry far more than Mike Forbes had.

They decided to get married at St. Peter's church rather than at Greg and Julie's local church where Georgina's former marriage had taken place.

The wedding guest list featured so many of the people you have encountered in this story.

Mrs. Mary Brown, Georgina's former headmistress, was invited. She was so proud of what her former pupil had achieved. She had followed the news of Georgina's heroics in facing a pupil with a loaded gun.

Jennifer Hurst of the Shining Haven was making one of her rare visits to England and was also pleased to be included on the guest list.

Arthur and Georgina were really delighted to be able to introduce these special people from their pasts to each other.

Jo Smith, Georgina's line manager and her husband, were there of course.

How often we encounter common acquaintances and are brought to the realization of what a small world we live in. By a strange chance, Kathleen, who was Georgina's chief bride's-maid, had changed her job and had met and was engaged to be married to Georgina's former boyfriend, Jacob. He was also in attendance at the wedding.

Arthur's Cambridge friends were there, Paul and Helen, and Arnold and Alice. Paul was now a vicar in a Midland parish. Helen was interrupting her career to look after their two young children. Arnold was now a prosperous chartered accountant, working at a prestigious London firm. Arnold and Alice had three children, twin girls and a boy.

Ben, the head of physics at Kelvinborough School, was Arthur's best man. Ben and Jane had smiled at each other when they discovered the match they believed was made in heaven but which appeared to have foundered on the way, was actually going to take place.

Congratulatory cards were received from Ken who would always hold a special place in his heart for Georgina, and from Mr. Bronson. He was aware more than most, of how important Georgina's coolness and courage had been in upholding the reputation of Kelvinborugh School

Surprise, surprise, a congratulatory card was also received from Stinky! He was unaware of the part Georgina had played in exposing his examination paper scam but he knew that he owed his life to Georgina's courageous action.

After three years of marriage, Arthur and Georgina had a son. Georgina took a long career break at this point. A daughter followed three years later.

Arthur is now head teacher of a prestigious public school. The family attend church together where both Arthur and Georgina are licensed Readers (lay ministers). The tumultuous ride Arthur and Georgina experienced in the early part of their relationship has now been resolved into a blissful time of purposeful activity and fulfilment.